# LIFE IS A SPECIAL OPERATION

.com

# America 1$^{st}$

An

Unconventional

Short Story

by

Life is a Special Operation.com

America 1$^{st}$ / Paperback -- 1st ed.
ISBN: 978-1-946373-09-0
$13.99

# Contents

## Prologue: The Critical Question

**What would you do if you had the rest of your life to change your world?**

That's the critical question.

Not many people ask themselves this question. But we all could, and should.

This story is about an extraordinary man who has asked and answered this critical question several times in his life.

The first time he asked himself the critical question, he dedicated his life to fighting injustice and combatting terrorism.

The last time he asked himself the critical question ... well, we'll get into that in a few pages.

Our story begins in a blacked-out helicopter flying over the jungles of Colombia. The aircraft is full of bullet holes, leaking fuel, and the pilots aren't sure they will make it back to base. It's Joshua Stone's last day of war.

But before we join him during his last day of war, I want to give you a small glimpse into the depth of his character by flashing back to Joshua's first day of war.

### 1.  *Joshua Stone's First Day of War*

While we often work with all our resolve to build for our-selves and our loved ones a safe and secure future, life events, chance, and unforeseen circumstances have a tendency to take us in unpredictable directions. This is exactly what happened to Joshua Stone.

Since a young boy, Joshua was motivated to make a difference: to change the world and leave it a better place. Before he could even drive a car, he decided that the best way for him to help others would be to serve as a soldier—more specifically, as an Army Officer.

He therefore spent most of the days of his youth preparing and training for the Army and for war: he joined the chess team, played after-school sports, earned his Eagle Scout, attended the Virginia Military Institute and the Officer's Basic Course, spent a year in Korea, joined Special Forces and went to Ranger School and Scuba School. Despite all his preparations, his first day of war took him in an unexpected direction …

He was a junior Captain, a fresh graduate of the U.S. Army Special Forces Qualification course, strong and fit, well trained and handsome. Like everyone who endured such rigorous training, he was very confident, perhaps seeming arrogant to some.

Recently assigned to the 7th Special Forces Group at Ft Bragg, North Carolina, Joshua drove up to D.C. the night before so he could attend an entire day of intelligence threat briefs at the Pentagon. Of all the days in the world, it had to be that fateful Tuesday, September 11, 2001.

It took several minutes to get from his parking spot to the visitor's entrance. After verifying his Top-Secret clearance and going through a metal detector, the security guards finally allowed Joshua to enter the Pentagon.

*Enormous. Impressive. Thankfully, there is such good security,* he thought. *What a fortress.*

Joshua arrived at the conference room where he would be spending the rest of the day. It was a small room, complete with a rectangular dark wood table surrounded by ten leather rolling chairs, a computer desk, four chairs in the back of the room, and a projector hanging from the ceiling.

Although seven minutes early, Dr. Stephen Abduman welcomed Joshua to the briefing, ushered him to the empty seat at the far end of the conference table, and announced that they could "finally start."

Walking to his seat, Joshua locked eyes with another Special Forces Officer sitting in the chair next to his.

"Randy, wow! What a small world," whispered Joshua as he sat down.

"Joshua, Brother, great to see you," replied Randy Mullins.

Joshua and Randy were good buddies from the Special Operations Qualification Course, a one-year training pipeline designed to produce the smartest and toughest soldiers in the Army's arsenal.

"Let's catch up after lunch."

"Agreed."

The subject of the first brief was the Al-Qaeda threat. Dr. Stephen Abduman, a career intel analyst, proved himself a real expert. Because the briefing was top secret, no one was allowed to take notes. Joshua focused on every word.

About an hour later, the door swung open and a man entered in a panic. Joshua could see from his Army Branch Insignia that he was an intelligence officer, a Colonel.

"Dr. Abduman, we need you right now in the command center. A plane just crashed into the World Trade Center, and we think it was a terrorist attack. Let's go."

The two men disappeared into the hallway and the door shut behind them with a loud clunk. Everyone was speechless.

Master Sergeant Jones, the highest ranking and most experienced of the remaining briefers, hesitated for a few seconds, then shifted over to the computer desk.

"Let's take a break and see what's on the news."

No one disagreed.

It took a few minutes for MSG Jones to switch the computer system off and turn the cable television on. Four minutes later, the news reported a second aircraft crashing into the World Trade Center.

"It's a terrorist attack," interjected Joshua, breaking the silence. "One crash is likely a terrorist attack … but it's possible that it was just an accident. But two crashes—for sure this is a terrorist attack."

*This changes everything,* thought Joshua. He continued out loud. "We are now at war. This is going to be a pivotal moment for every American. And for sure everyone in this room."

For the next several minutes, everyone was restlessly glued to the newscast. Almost no new information was reported. The images of the burning buildings were becoming permanently etched within the minds of all.

Joshua thought, *Those cowards. Killing so many innocent people. At least I am in a position to fight back. They will regret this.*

Then the room exploded.

As with so many life-changing events, it happened in surreal slow motion.

The sound of the explosion passed its way through the building.

The force of the explosion blew everyone out of their chairs.

The fire.

The smell of the explosion.

The taste of blood.

The heat.

Joshua's last memory was noticing how loud the ringing was in his ears as he lay there, numb, trapped.

With no idea what just happened, he just laid there, vulnerable, confused, and afraid, until he passed out.

When Joshua woke up two weeks later, he wished he had hadn't woken up at all. Six broken ribs, second- and third-degree burns on his arms and back, a traumatic brain injury, a broken femur and major smoke inhalation.

He spent the next seven months at Walter Reed Military Hospital. It wasn't so nice back then, but at least he would be able to heal up and get back to work.

Many people would have considered seven months in an Army Hospital wasted time. But it was there that Joshua ran into another wounded warrior, one who would eventually become Joshua's best friend, battle buddy, and better yet, another brother.

## 2. *A Brotherhood is Formed*

By the time Joshua was on his way to recovering from his more severe injuries, it was time for him to do physical therapy to begin walking again. He was reassigned to the physical therapy ward, where he had a strict regimen of pool exercises, stretching, and light weights.

About the time that Joshua progressed to taking a dozen steps with crutches, he was told that he would be getting a roommate, another Special Forces soldier, Sergeant First Class Michael Campos.

Michael was lying in a hospital bed when they rolled him into Joshua's room.

"Hey, Sergeant, welcome to the physical therapy ward. I'm Joshua Stone. Nice to meet you."

"Mike Campos. Nice to meet you, too, Cappy." Mike had already done his homework to learn that his new roommate would be a Captain. For some reason he thought it was fun to call Captains "Cappy."

"How long have you been here?" Mike asked.

"Too long. But for sure I got another few months before parole. I guess I'll be your sponsor and show you around."

"No need right now," retorted Mike. "I can't do anything except lie here. It's going to be a few weeks before I can upgrade to a wheelchair, and the doctors aren't even sure I'll ever walk again … but I will. How's the food?"

"Not bad."

"Good to hear, Cappy. To be honest, I've been told this place is a real torture chamber and that I should think of it as Survival (SERE) school, with only slightly better food."

Mike started to laugh. It caught Joshua by surprise and caused Joshua to laugh, too.

Mike's laugh was so unique, so genuine, so innocent—like a mischievous school boy who just got away with stealing cookies from the cookie jar.

*Despite being so badly broken,* thought Joshua, *whoever this new roommate is, at least he has a good sense of humor.*

In contrast with Joshua, who was clean-cut, lean and handsome, Michael was short and stocky, built like a fire hydrant. Even before his accident, he always looked a bit disheveled. His hair always seemed to be out of place. And when he wasn't in uniform, he was only seen in a t-shirt and baseball cap honoring one of Ohio's collegiate or professional sports dynasties. Both of Mike's parents were doctors in Columbus, gynecologists to be exact. But Mike wanted a bit more action in his life than the family OBGYN practice could promise. After earning his bachelor's in international relations and a master's in business administration, Mike took his superior education and enlisted in the Infantry. No one in Mike's family was surprised or disappointed. Mike always wanted to be a soldier. They were, however, shocked that he enlisted for a three-year contract with the 1ˢᵗ Ranger Battalion at Hunter Army Airfield in Savannah, Georgia, and then reenlisted to go through Special Forces training and became a medic.

After only six months on a Special Forces team, young Sergeant Mike Campos graduated from SCUBA school and was promoted to Staff Sergeant. His duties didn't change, but it was a nice pay raise.

About a week after his promotion, Mike's team was conducting some advanced nighttime training at a Fort Bragg "urban operations" training facility. After fast-roping onto the roof of a two-story building, their helicopter had a catastrophic malfunction and crashed onto the roof. Both pilots were badly injured. One Special Forces soldier was killed instantly by the tail rotor, and Mike was ejected off the roof and fell two stories into the middle of the street below.

The team's senior medic discovered Mike lying on his back, without a pulse. He immediately started CPR, but it didn't work with Mike's body armor, helmet, and weapon strapped around his back. With a few slashes of his pocket knife, Mike was free of all his gear, lying in the middle of the street, and the senior medic restarted CPR. It was seventeen minutes before the medevac helicopter arrived at the remote training facility. They tried twice in the helicopter to revive Mike with the onboard automated external defibrillator (AED), and on the third attempt, his heart began to beat faintly.

He was flown directly to Duke University Medical Center, where he spent the next ten days in intensive care. The Army was so convinced that he was going to die that they decided to promote him to Sergeant First Class, something that Mike would later brag about during and after his recovery: "I was so squared away they promoted me to Staff Sergeant November first and to Sergeant First Class November thirteenth. At least they know how to recognize true talent." Of course, his mischievous laugh would follow.

As we all know, Michael didn't die. He loved life and fought hard to get it back. By the time he was pushed into Joshua's room, he had fought for every milestone that we all take for granted. His first milestone was to stay awake, conscious. Then he regained the strength to talk. Then to feed himself. Then to sit up in bed without help. By the time he met Joshua Stone, his goals were clear: wheelchair first, go to the bathroom by himself second, walk third. Once he could walk again, it would only be a matter of time before he returned to a Special Forces team. He could see the finish line, but the distance to get there was enormous.

Thankfully, Mike had just met the man who would push and encourage him back into health. A brother who would eventually share not just his hospital room, but also his life.

For the next few months, the two invalids were inseparable. More than once, Mike ended Joshua's pity party and more than a hundred times, Joshua ended Mike's. Helping Mike was a great way for Joshua to stop focusing on his own inner and outward struggles. The more he put into their friendship, the more they both healed.

Joshua was there when Mike pulled himself into a wheelchair for the first time, was there when he swam his first lap, and was there when he took his first step. But he was also there when Mike threw bedpans across the room and cried because his nerves were causing agonizing pain. Sadly, they had more bad times than good, but each day was one step closer to the goal of full recovery.

Joshua was discharged six months before Mike. But they kept in touch, and Joshua came up to visit every two or three weeks. Despite being gross violators of the officer-enlisted fraternization regulation, Joshua and Mike would remain partners in crime and brothers at arms for the rest of their lives. But when in the company of someone who cared, Mike always kept his military bearing, and "Joshua" turned into "Cappy" or "Sir."

Everyone but Joshua and Mike was surprised when Mike did return to Special Forces, where he was given a desk job in the basement vault of the Group's Operations Office for a year before being assigned as the junior medic to the same team as Joshua.

For the rest of his life, Mike would walk with a distinct hobble that you could recognize from a hundred meters away. Although he would never be able to run more than a 100-meter dash, Special Forces kept him on active duty because he could still outshoot almost anyone on the planet and was always the smartest man in the room.

Mike and Joshua had such a unique bond. Meeting in a hospital, they recovered from massive injuries together. They went on to serve together at three different levels: Team, Company, and Battalion. As their careers progressed and became entwined, so did their personal lives. Joshua was the best man at Mike's wedding. They shared holidays, birthdays, and baptisms. They were a match made not in heaven, but forged by the Army during hard times and war.

Tragedies are terrible ordeals. But sometimes they are the catalysts that forge the deepest of friendships and force your life in different, but greater, directions.

… … ….

*We can stop the background story here. That's a pretty good rollup of Joshua Stone. A survivor. A man of character and resolve. A loyal friend. A true patriot.*

*Let's move on to the rest of our story.*

## 3. *Joshua Stone's Last Day of War*

*Joshua's last day of war was one of the happiest days of his life. Not because it was wonderful in and of itself, but because it was the dawn of a great hope.*

*After fifteen years of war, he was days away from a peace and a joy that he had never dared to even hope for before. Although it took about a month to do all his retirement out-*

*processing, that hope was born the second he stepped off the helicopter in Colombia.*

... ... ....

It is 0445 in the morning. With the exception of a formation of three MH-60 Blackhawks flying under night-vision goggles, Colombia is pitch black and still asleep. The rotary blades of the helicopter are spinning so fast that they create a huge circular pattern of magnetic illumination at their tips. Their faint glow is barely visible with the naked eye.

The pilot and co-pilot of the third helicopter chatter anxiously on the headset, endlessly cycling though their emergency procedures. They had taken fire at the helicopter pick-up zone, or "PZ," and are losing fuel. They calculate and recalculate if they will have enough fuel to make it back to base. The co-pilot scrolls thru his computerized navi-system, marking flat spots in the mountains below them where they might be able to conduct an emergency landing if they do run out of fuel.

Lieutenant Colonel Joshua Stone unplugs his headset from the radio terminal. He can't do anything to help the pilots, so he cuts off the radio noise and decides to enjoy the fresh air and glimpses of triple-canopy mountaintops silhouetted against the night's sky.

After several enjoyable minutes of getting blasted by the hundred mile-an-hour wind coming through the open doors of the helicopter, the crew chief grabs Joshua by the shoulder of his uniform, pulls him closer, and screams at the top of his lungs into his ear: "Hey, Sir! Pilots say we're going to make it! Got about ten minutes of fuel left and the base is only four minutes away!"

Joshua nods his head in understanding.

*What a great way to finish ... and begin,* he thinks to himself as he goes back to enjoying the ride. His mind drifts back to his family, his future.

As soon as they land, seven men get out of each helicopter. Six are draped in muscles, jungle camouflage, nylon gear, communication cables, and carrying Army-issued assault rifles with sophisticated optics. The seventh man is their prisoner. The prisoners are barefoot, in handcuffs, and have pillowcases over their heads. Three *Policia* vans pull up to the landing zone, and each team with their respective prisoner gets into a van.

Joshua walks towards the hangar, nodding his head in approval to the soldiers driving away in the vans.

Once inside the hangar, Joshua is greeted by a dozen more men. He gives man-hugs to these teammates, one of whom is his long-time best friend, Mike Campos. Now a Command Sergeant Major, it is clear that Mike and Joshua still share a lot of love and respect.

"We finally got those dirtbags, Mike. Jackpot! What a great way to finish," Joshua announces.

Mike interrupts, "Whoa, Sir, you stink. You smell like a homeless man in July. Glad the mission was successful, but no more hugs and high fives till you clean up. Time for a shower."

As the Sergeant Major or 3rd Battalion, 7th Special Forces Group (Airborne), Michael Campos doesn't have time to be politically correct. He has to be direct and to the point. Commanding 600 of the world's toughest and most brilliant "criminals," as he calls them, required wisdom, common sense, a strong hand, and a very direct, hands-on approach. The boys loved him, as did Joshua.

Michael continues, "Hey boss, you need to hurry up, too. After your shower, we need to debrief you and put you on the rotator back to Florida. It leaves at 0800."

Despite knowing how stinky he must be after three days in the jungle, Joshua stops by the command post and gives an awkwardly long hug to the new Commander, Joshua's replacement and dear friend, Lieutenant Colonel Phil O'Connor. Joshua wraps his leg around Phil to get even closer, hoping the stink will transfer via osmosis onto Phil. This is classic Special Forces field humor, the kind that only is shared between men who have spent three days in the jungle without a shower. Phil shoves Joshua away.

"Thanks, Brother, that was the stinkiest man-hug I have ever had. I am going to have to throw away this uniform now. Jerk."

"Is that the response I get for mission success? I give you the best Battalion in the Army, and on your first week in country we capture the leaders of the number-one cartel in Colombia. You better come back and get some more stink hug."

"No, seriously, Joshua. You stink. Go clean up, and let's get to your debrief. Hopefully we will have time for one last coffee before you head back to Headquarters."

Phil was tall and lean, six feet and a 180 pounds. Although he was confident and spoke directly to the issue, Phil led by calculated decisions. From choosing his wife or deciding when and where to get his haircut, Phil thought through every decision he ever made. He was never selfish or ambitious, only using his rank and power to advocate for "the boys." This is what endeared Phil to his men and what solidified his friendship with Joshua twenty years ago while they were both Lieutenants in the 101ˢᵗ Airborne Division (Air Assault).

The funniest part about Phil was that everyone liked and respected him so much that they only referred to him by his two nicknames: "Phil" or "Fighting Phil." No one ever called him by his rank and last name, which was mandatory military protocol. It was always "Phil" or "Fighting Phil." As in …

"Who told you to do that, private?"

"Phil said I should do it, Sergeant Major."

"That's Lieutenant Colonel O'Connor to you, knucklehead."

"Yes, Sergeant Major. That's what I said. Phil told me to do it."

Joshua relents from his stinky man-hug and heads for the make-shift team room in the back of the bunker, where he locks up his M4 and systematically unloads the field gear from his rucksack.

As the outgoing Battalion Commander, Joshua had no business being on a tactical mission with a Special Force team, technically known as an Operational Detachment – Alpha or ODA. His time on a "team" doing tactical missions was over ten years ago. But Joshua had a special relationship with his current Battalion, former Company, and old team. Rare in Special Forces, Joshua was a Battalion, Company and Detachment Commander within the unit. That means he spent almost all of his career working, living, and fighting with the same men. His former team let Joshua go on the mission as a going-away present, a one-of-a-kind gift only given to a trusted friend and proven soldier of kindred spirits.

Joshua throws his entire uniform in the trash, including his boots and boonie cap. After a long, ice-cold shower, he puts on a polo, dress slacks, and wingtip boots, finishes packing his gear, and heads over to the conference room for his debrief.

Two hours later, Joshua comes out of the conference room. Mike intercepts him, and they walk back to Phil's office to enjoy some coffee and ten minutes of chit-chat before heading to the six-seater jet airplane parked in the adjacent hanger.

Joshua jumps aboard. It is a civilian-looking aircraft leased by Army Special Operations Command. The crew is all active duty. The premise is to look like rich civilians, not like U.S. Special Ops guys. It helps facilitate freedom of movement and Operations Security for the Special Operations Task Force (SOTF) fighting the dangerous war on drugs.

After a two-minute safety brief, the plane fires up, taxis to the north side of the airfield, and then takes off for Eglin Air Force Base, Florida, home of the 7th Special Forces Group (Airborne). Exhausted from his three-day mission and excited for the next phase of his life, Joshua falls asleep before the aircraft even takes off. He outwardly smiles as he dreams of his new life after retiring from the Army.

## 4.  *The Stone Family*

A few hours later, Joshua lands at Destin-Fort Walton Beach Airport and his plane taxis to a discreet, private hangar owned by U.S. Special Operations Command (USSOCOM) at the end of the runway.

As with all of Joshua's missions and deployments, he returns to no fanfare, no parade, no welcome-home ceremony. Just one "quiet professional" glad to have done his duty and thankful to still be alive.

No one ever would have guessed that earlier in the day, Joshua and his men invaded a heavily guarded fortress and captured not just the number-one drug trafficker in Colombia, but one of the evilest men on the planet.

Joshua is greeted inside the hangar by Specialist Hall, a young but squared-away medic assigned to the Battalion Aid Station. SPC Hall hands Joshua his cell phone and some mail, and directs him over to a customs agent who was also waiting for the plane's arrival. After a quick discussion with the customs agent, Joshua jumps into a government-owned minivan, and SPC Hall drives him back to the 7th Special Forces Group compound at Eglin Airforce Base. As soon as he gets in the van, Joshua calls his wife and lets her know she can pick him up at the office.

"Love you, too, Beautiful," Joshua ends the phone call. "See you in ten minutes."

Although it is a short drive from the airfield to the compound, Joshua's mind gets lost as he thinks about how much he loves his wife and is blessed to have her.

Many men say that their wives are their "better half"—in Joshua's case, it was true. Colette was the most wonderful and most remarkable woman in the world.

The astonishing story of their love is a fairy tale orchestrated by God Himself. But it is too long to tell right now.

Joshua and Colette met for "the first time" many times, before they finally had the eyes to see who was standing before them. But it was in Paris, seven years ago, that they "met" for the last time at a mutual friend's BBQ.

Joshua recognized immediately that Colette was exponentially out of his league. A few phone calls later, and he was in love. Joshua knew he was going to marry her before their first official date, and four weeks later, they were married.

Colette was such a polarizing figure. She was loved by those with a pure heart and hated by those without. She was petite and physically fragile, but strong in character and resolve. Half French, half Mexican, she was absolutely gorgeous. She was very dark as a child, something which made her even more of an outcast in her small village outside of Versailles, France. French and Spanish were the languages she spoke at home. As an adult, she developed a lighter complexion. Her long dark hair now had chocolate and honey highlights, and her eyes were always ablaze with intelligence, dark and mysterious. The more you studied her eyes, the more they remained out of focus and out of touch. Joshua called them "unknowable."

Friends and family were all mad that Joshua and Colette eloped without inviting anyone to share in the ceremony. But this was not their way. Having waited so long to find each other, they didn't want to delay any longer, and certainly not for something as inconsequential as a big ceremony.

Eleven months after getting married, they had a son, Jacob. He was such a delight and the object of such joy. Full of curiosity, he loved to ask questions and learn. He was especially fond of putting things together. Toy log cabins, Legos and puzzles were always his favorite games.

Even now, Joshua is ten times more in love than when they were married, and he considers himself the most blessed man on the planet.

## 5. *The 7ᵗʰ Special Forces Group (Airborne)*

About a month after leaving Colombia, Joshua is "front and center" before a crowd of 400 men at his retirement ceremony. As you would expect from any event that Joshua had to plan himself, the celebration is catered by his favorite Mexican food restaurant. As a Mexican food snob and a self-proclaimed "greedy rat," Joshua made sure that he brought all the spare Tupperware from his house, hoping to be able to feast on leftovers for two or three days after the ceremony.

The 7th Special Forces Group Commander, Colonel John Morrison, gives Joshua his retirement award, a Legion of Merit, and says several nice things about him.

"We are absolutely going to miss this exceptional Officer and man. Joshua has this amazing ability to see the big picture, to understand how it works, reverse engineer the processes, and make it even better. If ever there was a man I could trust to do anything it in the world, it would be Joshua. If he gave me his word he would do it, then in my mind it was already done. I love and respect this man, and will desperately miss him."

Although their relationship had a rough beginning, John Morrison and Joshua had a profound respect and trust for each other. Straight out of Walter Reed Hospital, Joshua reported back into the 7th Special Forces Group (Airborne) and to his company commander, then Major John Morrison. Morrison immediately began to cuss him up and down, threatening to fire him if he made one single mistake. So much for a gentle "welcome home." It took a few months, but Joshua eventually earned his boss' trust and friendship.

All Special Forces Officers are men of strong character. But John Morrison was exceptional. Because Morrison's father was a case officer with the CIA, he grew up in Europe, moving from country to country every few years. He was tough and explained that this toughness was developed as a kid who refused to be picked on as the new guy with the funny accent at all the schools he attended over the years. As a child, change and culture shock were his constant companions. He finally stabilized for three years at a Swiss boarding school before going to West Point for four. Serving as the 7th Group Commander in Florida, COL Morrison's house was his eighteenth residence while on active duty and the thirty-first place he lived in his life. He was a patriotic gypsy without roots, only a lifetime of service and sacrifice. He was polished when he needed to be, but his normal disposition was to be a confrontational jerk. He loved the conflict. Asking Colonel Morrison to hold back his opinion is like asking water to stop being wet.

In true fashion, COL Morrison reminds the room that he is absolutely against Joshua retiring. He adds that Joshua should stay in the military because the world needs a leader like him.

All of Joshua's Special Forces colleagues are glad to see Joshua so happy but sad to see him go. Phil and Mike flew up for the ceremony. They wish him well and also say nice things about him during the ceremony.

Joshua thanks the crowd for coming to his retirement ceremony and begins his remarks by thanking his wife, Colette, for her love and support during the final years of his career. He highlights how honored he was to have been able to serve with and command such amazing men, specifically mentioning his "Ranger Buddy" and best friend Sergeant Major Mike Campos. He then finishes his short speech by announcing that he just accepted a nine-to-five job teaching American government at the University of Arizona and that he is looking forward to spending all his free time and summers with his wife and son. He also mentions his plans to upgrade the family cabin with Jacob.

Colette and Jacob, now six years old, are sitting in the front row of the auditorium for the ceremony. At the end of the ceremony, Colette is given a dozen yellow roses to thank her for her service and for supporting her husband and the Special Forces community. Both Colette and Jacob are glowing, so happy and so proud.

## 6.  Back in Arizona

As Joshua and Collette snuggle on the couch in their new home in Tucson, Joshua feels a peace and hope that he has never felt before, something he never dared to allow himself to feel while still serving in uniform.

Born in Belgium while the Stones were stationed at NATO Headquarters, Jacob spent the first half of his life in Europe and the second half at Eglin Air Force Base, Florida. This new Tucson house will be his permanent one. The entire family is anxious to settle down and establish roots. Joshua and Colette always loved to visit Tucson. They love the mountains, the dry heat, the Mexican food, the sunsets, and the wildlife.

During their first visit to Arizona after Jacob was born, the three of them took a few days to visit the Grand Canyon. While exploring, they stumbled upon an old cabin for sale in the woods outside of Flagstaff, Arizona. They bought it immediately and have enjoyed the prospect of "working on it" in their spare time. Visiting the cabin was more like camping than like staying at a hotel or a civilized house, so it was always such an adventure to drive up to the cabin.

Now, Jacob has two homes in Arizona. What more could a boy ever hope for? Jacob is the happiest kid you could imagine. And yet, his happiness isn't a fraction of his father's happiness.

With moving day behind them, their new home is in complete disarray. Unpacked boxes are everywhere. Joshua and Colette snuggle on the couch as they enjoy the sunset. She leaves the room for a minute and reappears with a present.

"Professor Stone," she says, "I want you looking tip-top at your new job. Happy retirement present."

He unwraps it: a fountain pen, a writing tablet, and a weekender suitcase. They kiss.

"I have one more present for you …" she continues, and whispers the rest of her gift into his ear.

Joshua looks down at her stomach and smiles. Tears of joy immediately begin to trickle down his face. His kisses her gently, holds her tightly, and thanks God silently.

A few minutes later, Jacob jumps onto the couch and perfects the happy and sentimental moment. The four of them hug.

*This moment. Right now,* thinks Joshua, *is the happiest and most hopeful moment of my life.*

## 7.    The First Day of the Rest of Joshua's Life

The next day, the Stone family sleeps in.

After breakfast burritos and cappuccinos, Jacob goes into his room to start unpacking his toys. Colette and Joshua start unpacking the boxes in the kitchen. After unpacking most of the kitchen, Joshua takes a break on the couch. Colette joins him. They snuggle in, laying on their sides, face to face. They kiss. In such a state of peace and happiness, Joshua falls asleep.

About an hour later, Joshua wakes up to an empty house. He finds a note on the kitchen counter: "Love you, sleepyhead. Taking Jacob to the supermarket to get some groceries. Be back soon."

Joshua gets to work unpacking boxes.

A few hours later, two police officers pull up Joshua's driveway. A seasoned vet and a rookie straight out of the police academy, the two decide that the young officer will take lead on this case. He knocks on the door.

Officer Gomez hesitates. "There has been a terrible accident."

He explains to Joshua that someone ran a red light and T-boned his wife and son.

"It looks like they died instantly."

It was a hit and run. The police think it was a drunk driver.

Although no stranger to death and tragedy, Joshua is absolutely unprepared for this terrible news.

His ears begin to ring. He begins to smell fire, to feel the heat.

Although he knows he is not back in the Pentagon, his mind wanders.

He is done, lost in thought.

The world disappears.

The police give him a few minutes and gently talk him back into reality. They eventually ask if they can escort him to the morgue to identify the bodies.

The only way to the morgue is through the very intersection where the accident took place. As they awkwardly wait at the traffic light, Joshua unclips his seatbelt and gets out. Crew members are sweeping up broken glass. Colette's car is still upside down at the bottom of the hill just across from the intersection. A tow truck is trying to winch it up so he can take it to the impound yard.

Joshua stumbles around the crash site, oblivious to the cars and spectators, neglecting his own safety. One of the cleanup crew pulls Joshua onto the sidewalk and yells at him for not paying attention to the traffic.

Officer Gomez finally corrals Joshua back into the police car and they continue on to the morgue.

After identifying the bodies, Joshua requests a few minutes to say his last goodbyes. After two hours, Officer Gomez reappears and gently pulls Joshua away from his loved ones.

This is the worse day of his life.

Every second an hour. Each minute a day. These hours pass like weeks of torment. Joshua is numb. His ears still ring. The police have to say everything to him two or three times to get a response. He is speechless.

## 8.   Evil Paparazzi

It is late afternoon when Joshua finishes all the paperwork and Officer Gomez drives Joshua back to his house. The drive is awkwardly silent. About a dozen reporters and cameramen are at the end of Joshua's driveway.

*Vultures!* he thinks to himself.

The police officer drives past the crowd and stops at the front door.

Joshua jumps out of the car and aggressively walks back to the journalists. Despite being enraged, he just wants to scream at them, to get their venom off his chest and their bodies off his property.

"Sir."

"Sir."

"Over here."

"Can you tell us how you feel?"

"Is it true …"

Anger courses through his blood. Joshua can hardly speak. And for sure his can't put together the severity of his feelings and pain.

"SHAME ON YOU!"

"VULTURES!

PIGS!"

"GET OFF MY PROPERTY RIGHT NOW!"

Enraged, Joshua turns and walks back towards his house. The reporters didn't get it. Joshua's words were wasted on most of the vultures standing at the end of his driveway.

"Sir …"

"Please."

"Can you give us a bit more detail about the accident …?"

"Any leads on the drunk driver?"

Realizing that Joshua is not coming back, reporters and crews quietly grumble to themselves as they pack up and leave. Only, Priscilla Kartoff from channel 4 news and her camera man remain.

Speechless. She sits down on the curb and starts to think about what she is doing there.

"That guy is right," she reflectively admits to her camera man. "This is not why I got into journalism. I've changed. This is not who I want to be. I have to do something else."

## 9.  *Pain & Rage*

Around eight p.m. that evening, the same two officers return to Joshua's house.

The neighbors called the police and reported that they heard screaming and crashing furniture. They were afraid of vandalism. As it turns out, it was only a man screaming out his pain after having lost in the same day those he loved most.

After several doorbell rings, no one comes to the door. The police walk around the house to find that the back doors are open.

The house is in the kind of disarray you would expect from a place the day after a move, except that a couch is flipped into the corner of the kitchen and a dining room chair is lodged into the ceiling. Joshua is sleeping on the floor in the living room, completely sober, but drunk with sadness and exhaustion.

The police wake him up. He is different now. Silent. Voiceless from screaming. Broken.

Joshua whispers to the police, assuring them that he is not a threat to anyone and just grieving.

Joshua gets a ticket for disturbing the peace.

## 10. *The Funeral*

The funeral is in Tucson. It is a complete family reunion of sadness. It's raining. The chapel is filled, standing room only. Joshua wants nothing more than to be left alone. But he is wise enough to know that his friends and family also needed to mourn and have closure.

Joshua's older brother, Noah, is the presiding minister. Although they are two years apart, everyone always said they looked like twins. Not anymore. Sixteen years of war has taken its toll on Joshua's body. Not to mention that the past week added ten years onto Joshua's face and eyes. Noah looks a decade younger.

The two brothers still bear a strong resemblance. Noah is a few pounds heavier, since he wasn't required to remain in world-class shape for his service, and his hair was curly and a bit messy. Both men were academics and introverts by nature, forced to be charismatic when needed to satisfy the requirements of their chosen professions.

Like Joshua, Noah is very intense. He always makes invasive eye contact, is an active listener, asks the hard questions, and is absolutely afraid of nothing and no one. He takes his calling as a minister very seriously and uses every opportunity he has to explain biblical truth or the love of God.

Although Joshua wants the service to be over, he knows that Noah is going to make it an opportunity to give a theology class to the entire family and all their friends.

Noah reminds everyone at the funeral that contrary to popular misconceptions, the dead are not tormented by everlasting fire, they are not in purgatory working out their salvation, and they are not in heaven floating on clouds like angelic fat kids with wings and bows and arrows.

The entire front facade of the chapel is glass, revealing a spectacular view of the Catalina Foothills. What an amazing view of God's majesty, made even greater when juxtaposed with the sadness and finality of the two closed caskets in the foreground.

There is a reception after the funeral in the adjacent building. It is another mechanism to prolong Joshua's pain. With every conversation he has, with every condolence he receives, Joshua sinks deeper and deeper into a black hole of sorrow.

As the reception is nearing its end, Sergeant Major Mike Campos and seven other men pull Joshua aside. Joshua is surprised that all his original teammates made it to the funeral. He greets them all by name and gives them heartfelt hugs. Three men are still in uniform, and the four out of uniform look like retired linebackers. These men represent the remaining soldiers still alive from Joshua and Mike's original team, Special Forces Operational Detachment–Alpha 785.

Mike whispers something in Joshua's ear, then gives him a folded white sheet of paper with a name and address. Joshua discreetly puts it in his pocket. He then looks up and makes eye contact with each one of his old teammates. They subtly nod their heads up and down, and then reverentially disperse.

## 11. Back to the Critical Question

Noah Stone pulls up the driveway and into Joshua's garage. He decides that it is a good idea to keep his brother company for a few minutes before driving down the street to his house, where his wife and kids are also ministering to grieving family members.

Joshua tries to send Noah home, but Noah invites himself in and pours them both a glass of red wine. They walk outside and sit on the porch swing.

The two brothers sit in silence as they take in the spectacular golden sunset.

Noah breaks the silence. "Remember how Dad used to always say that the big Stones must help the little Stones?"

"Of course."

"Well, Brother, thanks for being the big Stone and taking care of the rest of us. I'm the minister with all the answers. But you are the biggest Stone the family ever produced. Thanks for always holding us together and for being so strong for us. I'm sure that you are going to be strong for all of us again in the near future. But in the meantime, please let us help you."

Noah continues. "I am going to let you have a little time and space. But we are going to come over frequently to check in on you. We're going to make you spend time with us. Because for sure, you can't get through this on your own. Okay?"

No answer.

"Okay? Hello, anyone out there?"

"Yeah, yeah, yeah. I got it. You're welcome and thank you. But don't worry about me. I'll be fine. I just need some time to figure it all out. Don't worry, I'm not going to do anything stupid."

"And that, Brother, brings up the critical question," replies Noah. "What are you going to do now?"

They sit in silence. About a minute later, Joshua finally answers.

"I don't know, yet. For the first time in my life, I just don't know."

## 12. Local Channel 4 News Report

"After a career of war, a local hero returns home to the greatest tragedy of his life. One of Tucson's own, Joshua Stone, spent the last twenty years of his life in the Army. Injured in the September eleventh attack on the Pentagon, Joshua got healthy again and then spent the next sixteen years fighting terrorists and narco-traffickers in the global wars against terror and drugs. Just days into his retirement, his wife and six-year-old son were killed last week in a hit and run. Police suspect a drunk driver. Even in the midst of his sorrow, Joshua tried but was unable to make a statement."

They show a clip of Joshua crying, turning his face, and walking back to his house.

"Our hearts and thoughts are with him today."

## 13. Planning: E - 30 Months & Counting

Joshua is sitting on the same couch where he and his wife snuggled just six days earlier. The folded white sheet of paper that Mike gave him is on the coffee table next to his notebook, new fountain pen, and his bible.

Joshua starts writing in his notebook. Over the next few days, he barely moves from the couch.

He is almost silent, as if he can't talk anymore. When Joshua does talk, it is always in a whisper and only when absolutely needed.

## 14. Summer School

A few weeks later, the University of Arizona summer school begins. Joshua thought about cancelling his six-week summer course, but he decided to be a man of his word and to finish what he promised.

He heads in early to swim some laps at the U of A pool. After a 2,000-meter morning PT (physical training) session, Joshua showers, gets dressed, and arrives to his classroom twenty minutes early.

The Tucson summer is in full swing, but still Joshua manages to wear a suit and tie. His beard, mostly silver with hints of red, is now a centimeter long. Despite being empty inside, Joshua looks the part of an engaging and elegant university professor.

By the time he finishes reviewing his notes, Joshua is standing in front of twenty-nine university students.

He begins the two-hour course by going over the syllabus and highlighting expectations. Joshua then asks each of the students to introduce themselves, taking mental notes as they talk. The students are arrayed in variations of shorts and t-shirts. Two of the ten ladies are wearing skirts. Four of the nineteen boys are wearing collars. No ties. Two are sophomores and the rest freshmen. Six chewing gum. All of them check their cell phones at least once in the ten-minute introduction period.

After their introductions are complete, Joshua begins his own introduction. He references the Virginia Military Institute, where he endured spartan, prison-like conditions for four years, went to classes six days a week, and graduated class valedictorian. He references his grad school work at Harvard, where he read on average 200 pages of homework every day. He references serving as an Army Special Forces Officer in over twenty countries, fighting the war on drugs, and the global war on terror.

Joshua finishes his personal introduction by saying, "I've had a very unique education experience, one which you guys can hardly imagine. I know this isn't Ranger School, Command and General Staff College, the Virginia Military Institute, or Harvard—but it is American Government 101 at the University of Arizona, during summer school, on a 110-degree day. You need to know that I am old school and that

I value learning, manners, and effort. Please don't use your cell phone while in class. Please don't dress like you are going to the beach. And please show up for my class prepared."

"With that said, let's get started with class. Who read the homework assignment for the first day? Raise your hand?"

No one raises their hand.

"Wow." *Lazy brats.* "No one did their homework for the first day of class. How many of you have read the U.S. Constitution? Raise your hand."

"Three." *That can't be*, Stone thought.

After berating the students, reminding them that they are in a university now, Joshua begins his standard discourse about the importance of the U.S. Constitutions. He repeats the Preamble by heart, something he memorized when in the seventh grade. He makes the class read the Constitution out loud, each student standing up, reading a paragraph, then passing the text to the next student. Rather than having a lively discussion, they spend most of class simply reading the Constitution.

*This is going to be a long summer.*

## 15. The Recruiter

After the first week of school is over, Joshua walks into the Tucson Army Recruiting Field Office.

He reads the Recruiter's name and rank from his uniform. "Hey, Sergeant Smith, good morning. My name is Joshua Stone, and I am a retired Special Forces Officer. I was an 18A Lieutenant Colonel. I retired about six weeks ago and want to know what I need to do to get back on active duty. A few things have changed now in my life, and I want to go back into the service."

"I bet a few things have changed, Sir. Bet the 'Missus' just learned that she can't stand being around you 24/7 and that she needs you to go back to the Army and get deployed right away. Am I right? Is it your wife pushing you back into active duty? Or you just can't get a regular job?"

Joshua's blood pressure begins to raise. *Is this guy stupid?*

Joshua choses to ignore SSG Smith's reply. "Do I need to fill out any forms? Do I simply fill out a DA Form-4187? Any help or a point in the right direction would be appreciated."

"Sir, not sure if you heard, but two weeks ago the Army announced a drawdown. They're cutting the Army by twenty percent in the next twelve months, starting with officers and senior NCOs. There is no chance of you getting back on active duty. None."

Joshua is taken aback. Not by the rude Staff Sergeant and his belligerent tone, but by what he said. Joshua asks for written proof, and the recruiter reluctantly pulls out the Department of the Army (DA) Message explaining the drawdown.

Joshua reads the message twice and then excuses himself.

"Sorry about the bad news, Sir. Don't worry. It happens a lot. You spend all those years deployed away. There is bound to be some friction in your marriage in the first few months after retirement. She'll come around one of these days. Bring her some flowers and don't forget to take her on date night. Rangers lead the way! Huah!"

*Idiot! Bad news and a slap in the face. Maybe I can get a parking ticket and a flat tire, too.*

## 16. Encouragement

Joshua is pulling into his driveway when his mother calls.

He takes the call on the Jeep's Bluetooth.

"Hi Mom, I'm in the car right now. Can you hear me alright?"

"Sure can. I haven't heard from you in a few days and just wanted to check in and give you some encouragement."

Joshua's mom was queen of the backhanded compliment. What she really meant was not that she wanted to give some encouragement, but that she wanted to give some criticism. Knowing how this worked, Joshua instinctively replies, "Thanks, Mom. I'm doing well. Don't need any encouragement right now."

"Of course you do. I just wanted to let you know that I love you and support you. No matter what."

"Thanks, Mom. That's nice of you. And of course, I know it."

"How is summer school going?"

"Funny enough, Mom, it's not going that well. Not sure I want to teach for the rest of my life."

"Oh, Sweetheart. Just give it some time. You'll hit your groove one of these days. But give it some time."

"Thanks, Mom."

"Who knows, maybe you'll fall in love with one of your students one day and get remarried, make me some more grandkids."

"Mom, I don't want to talk about this right now. But just for the record, my heart is with my wife. I'll never remarry."

"Joshua, Dear, I just want to see you happy again."

"Thanks, Mom. That is loving of you. I want to be happy again, too. I'm just not sure I ever will be. With or without Colette and Jacob and ..." Joshua stops. Tears start rolling down his face.

He continues. "Mom, thanks for your concern. Life is special. A gift. I know that. And I do enjoy so many things. But I'm pretty sure that teaching American government isn't one of them. I'll figure it out. Don't worry."

"Oh, I wish you never would have retired. Then my grandson would still be alive. Better to be far away at Fort Bragg or Eglin. At least then I could still visit him. Now I got nothing and my son is living a terribly sad life all alone."

"Mom, I need to let you go. Thanks for calling and thanks for the encouragement. I love you, too."

"Okay, son. I'm here if you ever need me. Love you. Praying for you."

*Talk about kicking someone while they're down,* thinks Joshua. *Thanks for the call.*

## 17. Final Exams

Had Joshua been a quitter, he would have long ago walked away from teaching summer school. But as a man of integrity, he finished what he started. He could have justified quitting and blamed it on the tragedy. But that was not his way. So he gave the class his full effort, but they gave back almost nothing.

Joshua was right about one thing, though: American Government 101 was a distraction. Sadly, it was another negative distraction, one which he could have gone without.

Three students showed a real interest in his course and went the extra mile. Joshua enjoyed mentoring these students. But they were not enough to convince Joshua to continue teaching for a second career.

All of the other students gave a half-hearted effort, at most. Two students dropped the course, two failed, five got D's, seventeen earned C's and the three students previously mentioned got A's.

When the department head questions the grade spread, Joshua gets defensive and says, "I literally had three students in the course who cared. Everyone else is a knucklehead who I should have failed. I spent so much time correcting punctuation and subject-verb agreement that I barely even criticized the ideas of their essays, if they had any."

*What a sad commentary on the future generation. Shame on their parents,* he thinks.

"Joshua," replies the department head, "I'm so sorry you had a bad experience. I'm convinced that the current disinterest is a result of a lack of faith in modern-day politicians, not a lack of faith in the potential of the U.S. government and its original documents."

Joshua agrees. "I am with you a hundred percent. The foundational documents of the U.S. government are the best around, full of potential. The Constitution gives us such an amazing framework. It is our representatives and politicians who have failed us. The twenty-four-hour news cycle has ruined us. The men and women who govern us are politicians, not leaders. No honorable and decent man in his right mind would put up with the cruelty of the current yearlong campaign process. It is way too undignified. So only those who love and feed off the publicity are the ones who can successfully finish the campaign trail.

"But we've known this for years," Joshua continues. "The real reason I can't keep teaching is because of the caliber of students. They're just different. And I don't want to lower my standards to satisfy theirs."

"Don't you think you are jumping to conclusions? Would you consider trying one more class, but during the regular school year?"

Shaking his head, no, Joshua graciously thanks the department head for the offer. "I just can't do it. Thank you again for all your help, and I really do apologize for resigning my professorship. It just wasn't the right fit for me."

*Can't waste my time teaching punctuation and grammar to ungrateful kids who never should have been allowed to graduate high school. I have bigger fish to fry.*

## *18. Moving On*

Joshua spends the majority of the next few days on the couch. Same clothes, same couch. The sun goes up and down. He just keeps sitting there thinking, writing in his notebook. On the morning of day three, he starts to send some emails and set things in motion.

Workers of all sorts come to the house over the next few days, but Joshua barely communicates with them. He has given them their orders and expects them to do what they were asked.

Joshua goes through a few of the boxes remaining in the living room. He makes two different piles. One pile is all of his

Army uniforms, gear, and memorabilia. The other is a stack of important papers.

Slowly the furniture starts to disappear as workers come in and remove it. They even take his laptop and cell phone. You can see that they are from a battered women's charity by the marking on the truck. Joshua signs a clipboard.

With the exception of a few favorite items in black, including the suit he wore to the funeral, Joshua even gives away his clothes.

The next day a crew from a storage company nicely organizes and puts all of the Army gear, memorabilia, and paperwork into three small boxes. Joshua gives a worker a couple hundred dollars and signs their clipboard. He sleeps on a small mattress on the floor of his empty house. The next morning, he throws the mattress, a blanket, and the weekender into the back of his Jeep Grand Cherokee and drives to Noah's house to say goodbye.

"What are you going to do?" Asks Noah.

"Change the world … But I'm going to start with America first."


## 19. Harvard Law School

Joshua walks into Samuel "Skip" Goldberg's office and thanks the professor for making time for him. The law professor looks confused as they shake hands.

Skip is the kind of old-school professional who is becoming rarer every day. Unless at the pool, the beach, or his favorite vacation spot of Lago di Como, Italy, Skip is in a suit and tie all day long. On weekends, by 0800 every morning, Skip is in leather dress shoes, a tie, and a button-up sweater. He is soft spoken, competent beyond belief, and gracious to the core.

Decades earlier, the Goldberg family endured a terrible tragedy. Skip's youngest daughter, then fourteen years old, was raped. Two weeks later, she killed herself. To make matters even worse, the judge found the sex offender "sick," not guilty, and after two years in a clinic for observation, the sex offender was back out on the street. It was such a terrible situation.

Besides being a great lawyer and gifted teacher, Joshua respected Professor Goldberg because he dedicated his life to justice, yet was denied it. This is why Joshua wants to speak to him, today. He needs to reflect on the nature of justice, and there is no one who better understands it than Skip Goldberg.

Knowing his "operational environment," Joshua also wears his dark suit and tie. But no matter how well-dressed he is, Joshua still cannot hide the sadness in his eyes.

"Joshua," Skip begins. "Please sit down. I remember you from class about ten or twelve years ago. Weren't you in the Army? Are you out now?"

Joshua quietly answers: "Great memory, Professor. I'm impressed. I was in your National Security Law course about ten years ago. I was in the Army then, but I retired three months ago."

"Congratulations on your retirement," Skip says. "How can I help you?"

Joshua reminds Skip that his secretary scheduled him for twenty minutes, and asks if he can actually have all twenty minutes. Skip looks at his watch and agrees. Joshua then starts asking the Professor about why he practices and teaches law.

After a few minutes, Joshua drops a bomb into the conversation by bringing up Skip's past. He does it mildly, but the explosion of a tragic memory never detonates as gently as desired.

The lawyer gets choked up and asks Joshua to leave. Joshua doesn't budge.

Professor Goldberg admits that the system has significant flaws, but that good men are needed to teach it, use it, and to work within it. The professor eventually loses his sad countenance and his normal, optimistic demeaner returns. He loves to talk about the amazing potential of the American justice system. Joshua is impressed that such a victim of the system can still find hope in the system.

Joshua puts a piece of paper down on the desk and asks the professor how much he charges by the hour.

The professor shakes his head and says that he rarely takes on casework these days. "Why do you ask?"

Joshua ignores his question and responds, "When was the last time you were in Tucson?"

The professor retorts defensively, "How did you know I was from Tucson?"

Joshua pulls out his ink pen and signs the contract he carried in with him. "It is easy to remember when your favorite law school professor is from your same hometown. I need your help next month for a few hours in court. Easy work. Three to four hours, max. I promise." Joshua places an envelope full of money on the table.

"This should cover your time, hotel and flight. The weather is perfect this time of year. Make a small vacation out of it. Enjoy some Mexican food. See family. Play golf at Saguaro Canyon."

Skip reads the document, asks a dozen more questions, and eventually signs the contract. He then calls in his secretary to make a copy of the contract for Joshua.

"No need to make a copy for me." interrupts Joshua. "I trust you."

They exchange pleasantries and Joshua leaves the office, nodding his head up and down as he walks towards his Jeep.

## 20. The Cabin

Joshua enters his dusty and neglected cabin in the pine forest outside of Flagstaff, Arizona, and throws his weekender on the floor. Dust goes everywhere, making its way into the fresh tears on his face, where it leaves a muddy trail of sadness.

He pulls a flashlight out of his pocket, walks into the underground cellar, and navigates the cobwebs to the corner, where he has a wine rack. He swings the wine rack out of the way and it reveals a four-foot-tall fireproof gun safe. Joshua opens the combination lock and pulls the door open to reveal an assault rifle, a hunting rifle, a tactical shot gun, 3 pistols, and ammunition for each. Joshua grabs the .22 pistol with silencer and places it on top of the safe. An old leather briefcase is on floor of the safe. It contains original birth certificates, marriage papers, and $25,000 in twenty-dollar bills. Joshua takes out a stack of twenties and closes the safe.

*Shopping time.*

Joshua jumps into the Jeep and drives to the local hardware store in town to get some cleaning supplies and construction materials. He spends the rest of the day cleaning the cabin and repairing holes in the roof.

## 21. Making a New Friend

The next morning, just after sunrise, Joshua is awoken by a terrible catfight in the backyard. He grabs his flashlight and heads over to investigate.

"Hey little buddy," he says as he approaches a baby cat lying on the ground at the base of one of the pine trees. As he gets closer, the cat doesn't run off.

*That's strange*, thinks Joshua. *He should have run away by now.*

Joshua squats down to get a closer look at the cat. He's a black cat, obviously feral, probably six to eight weeks old. Sadly, he's unconscious, but still breathing, with blood and bitemarks on his head and shoulder.

"My poor little brave one. Let's see what I can do to help you out."

Joshua takes the cat into the cabin, lays him on a blanket, then gets his first aid kit from the Jeep. He does his best to clean and flush the wounds, puts one stitch in the top of his head, cleans it all off with hydrogen peroxide, and then wraps his new friend in a blanket.

Joshua checks on him from time to time. But for the rest of the day, the cat does not regain consciousness.

*Not sure he is going to make it,* thinks Joshua. *But at least I tried.*

As the day comes to a close, Joshua fires up his camp stove and skillet, and he makes some beef tacos. He sits in his folding camp chair and enjoys the meal.

After watching the sunset, Joshua puts his plate on the floor and goes to get his mattress ready for sleep time.

When he comes back to the living room, Joshua is surprised to see that the cat is asleep on his blanket, but his plate has been licked clean.

*Looks like my little wounded warrior also likes tacos,* Joshua laughs to himself. *Hope it doesn't hurt his stomach. Should have put my plate up high. Tomorrow I will go get some cat food, and perhaps some proper furniture.*

The next morning, "Taco" is gone, but not before drinking the bowl of water Joshua left out for him.

## 22. Coffee Time

A few hours later, Joshua walks into the fanciest furniture and appliance shop in town and finds his way over to the coffee makers.

Although he prefers to never leave the house unless he is properly dressed and groomed, Joshua is still in his work clothes and is covered in dust from working at his cabin.

The head salesman looks Joshua up and down and says, "Excuse me, please don't touch that machine. It is very expensive."

*Yes, I know,* he thinks.

"If you are looking for a standard drip coffee maker, you are going to have to check out the supermarket across the street."

Joshua turns his attention from the coffee machine he is inspecting to the salesman. Looking directly into his eyes, he asks, "And your name is?"

"Florian," he replies with a confused look on his face, surprised at the eloquence of the man's voice and the intelligence in his eyes.

"Tell me, Florian, you get paid on commission, right?"

Florian's head nods up and down.

"You see, Florian, I know where the supermarket is. And yes, they do sell inexpensive coffee machines to people who have other priorities with their money. But I love good coffee and want to buy something fancy, expensive. But not from you. Because you are rude."

"So please go get your manager so I can tell him about your disrespectful arrogance … and please point another salesman my way. I want to spend a lot of money here, and I want them to get the commission, not you. Thank you."

After Joshua speaks with the manager, a new sales representative arrives to help him shop. She is absolutely gorgeous. Joshua doesn't notice. He buys a coffee maker, a twin bed, a leather couch, a coffee table, a dining room table with four chairs, and some kitchen supplies. He pays cash.

"Here's my address. Please have my furniture and coffee maker delivered next Monday morning."

"Sir, all of this is ready now and could be delivered tomorrow."

"No, thank you. Next Monday will be perfect. There is something I need to take care of in Tucson this week. But for sure, I will be back to the cabin on Monday."

## 23. To Kill or Let the System Work

Thanks to the white paper that Mike gave him at the funeral, Joshua knew his objective. But it was up to him to decide on the "task" and "purpose" of the mission. As always, he prepares well and rehearses thoroughly.

It is one in the morning on Interstate 10 between Phoenix and Tucson. With a backpack full of gear and a silenced pistol in the passenger's seat, Joshua is making his final approach. His mind is running full speed. The subject is an unusual one: justice, and what does it mean for him?

*Should I kill the man who killed my family? What good would it do? Would God forgive me? Could I live with myself? What if I just hurt him? Maim him? How do I get justice?*

*If the police find the killer of my family first, how long would he go to jail? Is it possible to get rehabilitated in prison? Or would he come out even more of a criminal? Maybe he would watch TV and lift weights all day. That wouldn't be a punishment at all. Would the police ever even find him?*

*I want justice. But even more so, I want my family back. And that won't happen anytime soon. So regardless of prison or death, what happens to the killer of my family will never bring me peace. So who even cares? I do!*

Joshua has already had this philosophical conversation in his head a hundred times. And each time he reached the same result: *I am a man of integrity who is deliberately living a life with purpose. I refuse to become anything less than my best. I will not make justice. But I will facilitate it.*

## 24. Justice

It's 2:30 in the morning, and Giovanni Chiamare, a twenty-five-year-old video game programmer, is asleep in bed. He wakes up to a burglar in his house. The burglar easily dominates him, subdues him, and then zip ties him to a chair. He can't move a muscle. The zip ties are so tight it hurts to breathe.

The burglar pulls out his cell phone and begins to record the interrogation. It doesn't take long before the man admits to doing the hit and run that killed Joshua's family. He says that he wasn't drunk, but he was texting. The burglar gets the man's cell phone from the nightstand and starts going through it. Sure enough, he was texting with his girlfriend at the time of the accident.

The burglar puts the barrel of his silenced pistol into the Texter's mouth, unwraps his Arabic style mask, and reveals his true identity.

The Texter, recognizing Joshua from the newspaper article about the car accident, pees himself and cries even more.

Joshua asks him why he shouldn't kill him.

The Texter is too scared to answer.

"No, seriously, Giovanni, tell me why I shouldn't kill you right now. Are you a good person? Do you do a lot of charity? Do you have big plans to make this world a better place?"

Again, the Texter is too scared to answer. They both remain in that awkward position for several minutes. The Texter's teeth chatter on the steel of the silencer.

Joshua eventually takes the unloaded airsoft pistol out of his prisoner's mouth and puts it back in his holster.

"Okay," Joshua whispers. "Check this out. I am not going to kill you … today. I believe that although you are a knuckle-head, and kind of a deadbeat, you are not a bad person. And for sure you're not a murderer. I believe that you were texting. I know you weren't planning to kill my family, but accidents happen. The bible even reminds us that accidents happen: 'We are all vulnerable to chance and unforeseen circumstances,' Ecclesiastes 9:11. But even though it was an accident, my pain remains. And that is why this situation is so terrible. You were being selfish and violated the law, which says that you should not text while driving. So you are going to have to suffer the consequences."

"I am going to give you two weeks to get your life in order … terminate your lease on this house, put your things in storage, quit your job, sell your car. Kiss loved ones goodbye and tell them you will only be in jail for a year or two. But two weeks from Monday, I want you to confess to the Tucson Police Department. Suffer the consequences of this stupid crime. And when you get out of prison, you better dedicate a small portion of your life to helping others. If not, I will find you, and I will finish what I have started today. Do you understand?"

The prisoner nods his head up and down.

Joshua cuts the Texter loose, then leaves through the patio door.

*Mission accomplished. Justice may never be done. But at least I tried to facilitate it, not make it.*

## 25. Furniture Arrives

Joshua opens the doors of his cabin with a smile.

"Thanks, guys, right on time."

Noticing they are both Latinos, he repeats himself in Spanish. They reply in perfect English, "I'm Juan and this is my colleague Jose. Nice to meet you, Sir. Looks like you have a furniture delivery."

"Please, bring it all in." One bed, one couch, one table, four chairs, and one top of the line coffee maker.

After they finish, Joshua invites them to stay for a coffee. They agree, and so he motions for them to wait on the new couch.

Joshua runs a huge extension cord from the coffee machine to his Jeep and plugs it in. It takes a few minutes, but eventually Joshua makes some cappuccinos. They sit down and enjoy the view.

"Looks like you have a friend," says Juan, the younger of the two workers, as he points to a stray cat hiding behind a tree in the back yard. "Does he have a name?"

"Taco."

"Cool name. Is he friendly?"

"Absolutely not. He's mean. I helped get him out of some trouble a few days ago. But I haven't been able to touch him since. He's pretty wild. You an animal lover?"

"Of course. My girlfriend and I love animals. We hope to get a big dog once we get married."

"Great. When will that be, Juan?"

"As soon as I can make enough money to support her. I'm a man, you know. I don't want my wife to work. I want to support her so she can raise our children. I'm just not there yet, financially." Changing the subject, he says, "So, you just moved here?"

"Not really, we bought this cabin several years ago. Thought it would be a nice project for my son and I to work on together."

"Oh … that's nice. But this isn't enough furniture for a family."

"No, it isn't … they were killed a couple months ago in a terrible accident. And I am just trying to keep myself busy as I figure out my plan for what I am going to do for the rest of my life."

## 26. Court

Professor Skip Goldberg stands up in court and explains that his client is devastated by the loss of his family. However, nothing will bring them back. Joshua will not press charges and requests that the judge be as lenient as possible.

The judge finds the accused guilty of accidental manslaughter and leaving the scene of a crime. He sentences the Texter to two years in prison and 1,000 hours of community service.

Sitting in the back of the courtroom, Joshua and the Texter exchange glances. The Texter panics but doesn't say anything. Joshua nods approvingly, then slips out of the courtroom.

## 27. The Cabin

Joshua finishes washing off in the stream. It is ice cold, but he endures it. He wraps himself in his sleeveless bathrobe, walks over to his Jeep, and starts it. Following the extension cord from the back door of his Jeep, Joshua walks into the cabin and flips on his cappuccino machine. After his coffee is ready, he turns off the Jeep and jumps onto the couch next to Taco, the cat. They enjoy the view.

After a few minutes, Joshua reaches over to pet Taco. He gets a slice in the hand and a great big hiss.

"Whoa, buddy. Got it. Guess we're not at that stage in our relationship yet."

After finishing his coffee, Joshua walks out the front door. The driveway is consumed by piles of rock, cement bags, logs, and a small camper refrigerator wired to two large solar panels.

"Okay. Time to get back to work."

## 28. Changing Jobs

The phone rings at the 3ʳᵈ Battalion, 7ᵗʰ Special Forces Group (Airborne) Headquarters. "Three-seven Sergeant Major."

"Mike, this is Joshua."

"Josh, how are you, Brother?"

"Been better. Good to hear your voice. How's Maria and the kids?"

"Yeah, yeah, yeah, they're great. I will give them your best. Listen man, I am glad you didn't kill that Giovanni kid. That shows a lot of character. I read in the paper that he turned himself in."

"Thanks for the intel tip. Turns out he is not a bad guy. Just made a bad decision. Don't forget, 'He who is without sin should cast the first stone.' Listen, this is my new cell number. Please don't give it to anyone except Phil, okay?"

"No problem. By the way, the boys miss you, but they are happy to be in good hands. Phil is still a superstar. Always thorough. Always the best. The boys are lucky to have had two great commanders in a row."

"That's good to hear. Thanks." Joshua continues. "Mike, I've got my plan together. It's a big one. I mean big time. It's ten years long … but the prep phase is only twenty-four more months. I can't tell you what it is right now … but I promise it is absolutely your cup of tea. I even think your wife will be happy."

"Okay, I trust you, boss. Let me know what you need."

"Mike, this is not what you want to hear, but I need a guy inside the U.S. Cyber Command and the Pentagon, and I prefer that it's you. Sorry about asking this of you. I know you want to stay at Group forever. But I know it will be worth it in the end. I need you to figure out how those places work. Cyber Command is about 30 miles northeast of DC. I recommend you get a place in the middle, but on the Maryland side of the border. I need you to do a year at each, but you need to start at Cyber Command. You think you can make that happen?"

"I can make anything happen, Joshua. But you owe me big time. You know that this is the best job in the world and that my family loves it here. They are going to be upset when I tell them we are moving to D.C. in the summer. Better be worth it."

"It is. Trust me."

"You know I always do."

## 29. The Crazy Environmentalist

Joshua wakes up with the sunrise. He slept well, but it is freezing inside his Jeep. He gets dressed, grabs his hygiene kit, and walks across the parking lot into the local coffeeshop. Jackson Hole, Wyoming is a beautiful place, but a bit too cold for sleeping in the Jeep.

*Tonight, I'll get a hotel room.*

After freshening up in the bathroom, Joshua looks, smells and feels great. Still mourning and still wearing variations of all black, the air of sadness is slowly lifting off of him. He enjoys a cappuccino as he reads through the notes in his journal.

About an hour later, a man in a tweed blazer walks in, looks around, and approaches Joshua. Joshua thanks him for coming and offers to buy the man breakfast. He accepts. They both order breakfast burritos and cappuccinos. Joshua thanks Lawrence Whitfield III for his time and hands him $1,000 in cash.

Known as "Scary Larry" to his friends and "Mr. Whitfield" to his clients, he was the former campaign manager of the Green Party, a pro-environment political party sponsored by several wealthy members of Greenpeace. When asked to meet Joshua, Scary Larry said he would do so for $200 an hour, but only for five hours. He agreed to meet between breakfast and lunch, so he could return to his real job in the afternoon.

What made Larry "scary" was his physique. He looked more like a body builder or a coal miner than a lawyer or political activist. Although he occasionally exercised, Larry was a huge man with impressive muscles. His shaved head, intense blue eyes, and ridiculously pointed nose never allowed you to be at ease around him. He is smart, passionate, intense. *Scary indeed.*

Mr. Whitfield is a lawyer by trade, but his passion is for protecting the environment. Having studied politics as an undergrad and law as a Rhodes Scholar, he decided in his early twenties that he would dedicate his life to protecting nature. The Green Party asked Mr. Whitfield to combine his passion with both sides of his education and help them run a campaign for the White House. Sadly, they failed miserably. But in doing so, they helped raise awareness of many issues that Mr. Whitfield held dear to his heart.

Joshua asks Larry about why the Green Party lost the last election. Larry is honest and straightforward. He is surprised that this visitor in front of him has such great questions. Being no stranger to smart environmentalists masquerading in organic clothes and long hair, Larry seems a bit surprised by the intelligence and intensity behind the man in black who obviously knew a lot about the US Government.

The two men discuss primary elections and why a third political party doesn't need to worry about the primaries. They discuss what it would take to get a third-party candidate's name onto the ballot in every state. Although Joshua knows most of the answers himself, he takes a few pages of notes during the conversation. He is pleasantly surprised by how smart Larry is.

Frequently, the conversation slips to the environment. Joshua allows the conversation to drift, even though he is paying for it, because it is fun to see Larry glow as he talks about cases where he protected the environment from the "government bastards."

Joshua talks about his cabin in the woods and how he loves living in the forest. Larry seems to know everything there is to know about the pine forests outside of Flagstaff.

At one p.m., Larry announces that he must get back to the office and invites Joshua for dinner. Joshua accepts, as long as they could spend a few minutes during dinner talking about solar panels and battery-powered houses. Larry smiles. He evidently knows a lot about environmentally friendly houses, as well.

Although Joshua paid for the introduction, a good friendship is growing.

## 30. Learning

Joshua walks into the dean's office at Northern Arizona University. Dr. Peter Garcia, affectionately known amongst the students as "Uncle Pete," is the favorite of all the students in the school, a real source of inspiration and help.

"Excuse me, Dr. Garcia, I have an appointment."

"Ahh, yes, Mr. Stone. Please come in. I make it a point to talk to every new student in the school. Especially old ones like you," he says with a warm smile. "Take a seat, please. Do you like coffee?"

Joshua begins to grin, but simultaneously sees the old-fashioned drip coffee machine in the corner of the room and disappointedly shakes his head no.

Five-foot-four, starched, ironed, and with shiny dress shoes, Uncle Peter looks more like a business executive than a dean of students. Joshua notices that the inside of his long sleeves were tucked in, rather than folded up, revealing amazingly tan arms but white hands.

*Eccentric,* thinks Joshua. *Looks like "Uncle Pete" plays golf.*

"So, tell me a little about yourself. Let me know what you want to get out of our school, and what we, as a school, can do to help you accomplish your goals."

"Well, Dr. Garcia, I like to keep to myself. So please don't expect me to say a lot right now. As far as classes go, I just signed up for a business class, an electrical engineering class, and Arabic. That's all. I have some ideas that will help a lot of people and thought it would be important for me to know how to start a business, do some electrical work, and say some key phrases in Arabic. I don't really need anything from you. It's just three classes."

"Okay, Mr. Stone, three classes are easy. But what's next? Do you want to get a bachelor's degree?"

Joshua smiles as he thinks back to his time at Harvard. He looks at the many diplomas on the dean's wall and decides to change the subject.

"Not really worried about getting a degree. But tell me about your degrees."

Uncle Peter quickly dismisses his pedigree, although it is very impressive, and starts a ten-minute discourse about how important education is and how he loves to help people learn and expand their minds.

Joshua asks Uncle Peter why he is at Northern Arizona University, despite his superior education and double PhDs.

Uncle Peter doesn't take offense, but he explains, "My goal is to educate, not become the Secretary of Education."

Joshua laughs, perhaps the first time in a month.

"I grew up in Arizona … love Arizona. And here I have free reign to make a difference. That is why this university has such a great reputation. We don't really care about conventional teaching models, which are recipes for mediocrity. We care about educating the next generation of fathers, mothers, leaders, teachers …"

For the second time in months, Joshua shakes his head up and down.

The two academics continue to talk for several more minutes. Uncle Peter is a rarity these days, a first-class educator with a passion for helping people accomplish their goals.

Despite being one of the oldest students in the school, Joshua is glad he decided to enroll. *It's never too late to keep learning.*

## 31. A Friendly Visit

An alert begins to beep on Joshua's phone. Setting his textbook aside, Joshua looks at his cell phone screen and smiles. He opens the security app linked to the camera at the entrance to his property. The camera reveals a minivan pulling up the driveway. It is his first face-to-face visitor since the funeral. Sergeant Major Mike Campos, his wife, and their seven- and eight-year-old sons come screaming down the driveway and park their rental van like they own the joint, a few inches from the front door.

Joshua is so happy they came to visit. He goes outside to welcome them. After hugs and a few tears, Mike passes on a message from their longtime friend: "Fighting Phil wanted me to make sure that you cut your hair and don't get fat."

They both laugh.

"Please tell Phil that he is a tool, and tell him not be jealous that my hair no longer has be in accordance with regulations."

Changing the subject, Joshua says, "Let's get some coffee."

Their jaws drop as they enter the cabin. Judging by the atrocious driveway and old, battered front façade of the cabin, no one would have thought that what lies within would be so remarkable. As soon as you step into the cabin, you are overwhelmed by the breathtaking view of the Rocky Mountains. The entire back wall is made of glass. Facing this view is the huge leather couch and a coffee table. Behind the couch is a table with four seats. And behind the table is a small kitchen with a ridiculously out-of-place coffee machine.

As the adults enjoy their cappuccinos, Joshua tells them about his plans to finish the bathroom, plumbing, and solar power systems. Phil asks about the college textbooks on the dining table. Joshua explains that he has a business idea, and that he is taking a business course, an electrical engineering course, and an Arabic refresher course at the local university.

"Thankfully, they have a great gym and indoor pool. I swim or lift almost every day. Plus, the locker room has warm showers."

Mike explains that his new job at Cyber Command is unlike any job he has ever had. "It's got a funny dynamic up there. I will show it to you when you come and visit. I don't run the place yet, but I'm figuring it out."

Joshua asks Mike's sons about their new school and life in Maryland.

They both like the area, but are glad to be visiting the Grand Canyon for spring break and to be away from all the traffic.

Mike agrees. "The traffic up there is killing me. Absolutely killing my spirit."

After an hour of catching up, Mike winks at his wife and then invites Joshua out front for some fresh air. As they walk to the back of the rental van, Joshua remarks about the two bikes suspended from the bike carrier.

"I am glad you like them," Mike interrupts. "They're yours."

Joshua looks at Mike with a curious expression.

"What do you mean, they're mine?"

"Well, I know you got the money. I know you are locked up here feeling sorry for yourself. And I know you could use the exercise. So, I took the liberty of getting you two great e-bikes and a bike carrier. That way when I come to visit, I can go riding with you."

"Are you serious?"

"Absolutely. Thankfully, you live in a part of the country where they still trust people at their word. Here is the receipt. The owner of the bike shop said you can stop by later this week to pay for the bikes."

"Eight thousand dollars! Are you out of your mind?"

"Hey, shut up tightwad. I got a killer deal on last year's model. Even got a military discount. These are the best bikes on the market. You'll thank me later."

After a few more minutes of yelling at each other, the two friends get on the bikes and go for an hour-long ride. Taco runs alongside them for the first few hundred meters, then pulls off to do something less taxing. Riding the e-bikes along the small roads of Joshua's neighborhood is such a treat. He is lucky to have such a crazy friend.

Joshua asks about the boys back at Group. Mike says they are all doing well and gives a by-name update on their favorite twenty guys.

"John Morrison has been promoted to Brigadier General and is now in charge of U.S. Army Special Operations Command. And Phil is doing well, as always, but mad that I had to leave for D.C. Whatever it is you got planned for me in Washington, it better be worth it, Josh!"

"Man, oh man," says Joshua. "Phil won't stop busting my chops. He called me twice this week to complain that you're gone. This project of mine is going to be worth it. It just needs a few more months to gain some momentum. I even have a job for Phil, if he would just shut up and stop complaining."

When the boys return from their bike ride, Maria and the kids are waiting outside. Setting the bikes against the side of the cabin, the men jump into the van and the five of them race off towards Flagstaff to go to Joshua's favorite steakhouse.

Mike insists that Joshua pay for steaks since he and Maria spent so much money flying to Flagstaff to see the Grand Canyon and check in on him. Joshua insists that Mike pay for dinner, since he, without permission, obligated Joshua for $8,000 worth of e-bikes. When the waitress brings the bill, both men smile and dig cash out of their pockets. Again, Joshua thinks how lucky he is to have such a good friend.

During the drive back to the cabin, Joshua smiles to himself as he reminisces about their friendship. Going through rehabilitation together; training together; deploying together; weddings; children.

Sadly, being around Maria and the boys makes Joshua miss his wife and son more than ever. Every day is a struggle to stay focused and to not feel sorry for himself.

After making plans to see each other in Washington, they exchange thank-yous and hugs, and the Campos family heads down the driveway.

"What a wonderful day," thinks Joshua as he waves goodbye and goes back into the cabin.

He freezes in shock.

It looks as if there was a pink explosion. Pink curtains are hanging over the windows. A pink blanket is draped across the couch. Pink pillows. Pink napkins. Pink towels. Maria and the boys had been busy "cleaning and redecorating" while the men were mountain biking. Taped to the coffee machine is a pink note. It reads:

"Thought you might need some groceries and a woman's help with the decorating ... we were right. Great seeing you today. Thanks for paying for dinner. We love you. Mike, Maria, and the Boyz. P.S. Don't forget to pay for the e-bikes tomorrow. Wouldn't want you to get a bad credit score!"

## 32. Starting a Business

The next morning, while enjoying coffee on the couch, Joshua calls an internet hosting company and pays for a web domain, www.America-1.com. He pays for it with an assumed name, using a prepaid Visa. The website is untraceable.

Joshua then pedals his new bike into town to the chamber of commerce where he starts a business called, "A1 LLC."

He then drives to the bank and opens a business account under the same name. While at the bank, he withdraws $8,500. He then swings by the bike store to pay for his e-bikes and buy a helmet.

## 33. Barbie Girl

A few days later, it is time for Joshua to do some grocery shopping. He jumps into his Jeep only to find that it has pink floor mats and a pink sun visor. He smiles.

"Looks like the Maria and the boys sabotaged my car, as well."

When he starts the vehicle, a loud song blazes on the CD player: "I'm a Barbie girl, in a Barbie world. I'm fantastic. Made of plastic…"

Joshua immediately skips the CD to the next song. But the same Barbie song starts anew. Joshua ejects the CD and throws it into the back of the Jeep.

*That's the last time I ever leave someone alone at the house.*

He smiles.

## 34. Brayden's Hardware

A crew arrives to the house the next morning in a white construction van with "Brayden's Hardware" written on both sides. It is a young crew, mostly nerdy white guys. Joshua only recognizes the driver, Juan, from his previous furniture delivery and invites them in for the customary cappuccino before they get to work. The rest of the crew agrees and files in.

"Juan, what're you doing here? Didn't you used to work for the furniture company?"

"Wow, thanks for remembering my name. Good memory. Yes, I did work for the furniture store in town, but Brayden's Hardware pays much better. I also have better benefits. Changing jobs was a no-brainer. You still got that mean cat, Enchilada?"

"Taco. And yes, he still hangs out. I can pet him now. But no one else can. I don't recommend you try."

The men spend the next few days rewiring Joshua's cabin and adding more panels to the solar configuration already on his roof. Joshua helps out so he can learn. They are happy to have the help.

Each day, Joshua welcomes them with coffee and breakfast burritos. He then rides off for a few hours of school. He returns in the early afternoon to help them finish their day.

After a week, the new system is complete. Solar panels charge a huge wall-mounted battery box during the day. Joshua then uses the batteries to power all of his appliances, lights, and of course, his e-bikes. If Joshua's batteries go dead, then the system automatically switches back to the Arizona power grid. With water from the stream and a battery-powered house, Joshua is happy to be living off the grid. He is also happy that he gets to test the system for a few weeks before heading to D.C.

## 35. The Drop Out

Joshua rides his e-bike to school for the last time.

After taking his finals, he thanks each of his professors for teaching him so much.

As Joshua is walking to his e-bike, Uncle Peter yells for him to stop and approaches quickly.

"Joshua, congratulations on finishing all of your classes. Where did you learn Arabic? Professor Abudib said you were her prized student."

"That's a long story, Dr. Garcia. I didn't always live in Flagstaff."

Uncle Peter waits for Joshua to further explain. But he doesn't. So he reanimates the conversation. "I just heard that you are not planning to take any classes next semester. Is everything all right? Can I help with anything?"

Joshua thanks the dean for being a good man and for caring about his students. He explains that like the dean, he is not interested in fancy diplomas anymore and that he literally took the classes so that he could learn more about starting a business.

Uncle Peter makes Joshua promise that if he ever needs anything related to education, he will call.

Joshua smiles and replies, "I promise, Dr. Garcia. If I need any educational help, you will be the first person I contact."

## 36. Inviting Himself Over

The phone rings.

"Sergeant Major, how may I help you?"

"Yes, I would like two ground beef tacos, a bean burrito, and a large Coke."

"Joshua, you knucklehead. Good to hear your voice. How are you doing?"

After some updates and small talk, Joshua gets to business.

"How do you like it up there, Mike?"

"Not at all. I miss the guys. The good thing is that I am learning a lot up here. No one knows how to deal with me, so I am kind of left to do what I think needs to be done."

"Thanks for doing this. I know you wanted to stay with the Battalion forever. I am coming for a visit. Two or three days. Can I sleep on the couch?"

"Of course. When?"

"Should take me a week to drive there."

## 37. The Jewelry Store

Joshua heads into town early the next morning to get some new tires for his Jeep and to buy a few groceries. While waiting for the tire guys to finish, he sees a Brayden's Hardware work van park across the parking lot. Juan jumps out and walks down a few doors of the strip mall to the jewelry store.

Joshua walks over and interrupts the window shopping: "Hey, Juan. What's up?"

"Oh, Joshua, you scared me. Guess I'm busted. I was just doing some dreaming. I can't wait to get married. About six more months and I will have enough money saved to buy a humble ring for my love."

"That's great, Juan. Tell me about her."

Juan explodes with praises and nice things to say about his dream girl. "I've loved her since we were thirteen, when I moved here from Nicaragua. But her dad refuses to let me marry her until I can prove that I can provide for her. I've got a steady job, I work hard. I have my own apartment now, and in six months, I should be able to buy that little stone over there in the corner for her."

Juan continues talking as Joshua's mind starts to get lost in the past… the moment when he proposed to Colette. It's a vivid daydream. She is standing next to their favorite picnic tree, not knowing what he is about to ask. Her hair is blowing in the wind, a little strand of hair in her face. He smells her perfume. It is as if there is no one around, just he and Colette, and her tears of joy when he looks into her eyes.

Woken up harshly from his beautiful daydream, Juan is asking Joshua for the third time if everything is okay.

"Of course I'm okay, Juan. I was just remembering that special moment. I will never forget it as long as I live."

Juan is a bit confused and asks, "The moment you bought her engagement ring? Did you also have to save up for a long time for a little stone?"

Joshua replies, almost laughing, "No, Juan, not the moment I bought the ring. I'm thinking of her reaction and how happy I was when she said yes."

"Hey Juan," Joshua continues, "I'm going out of town tomorrow morning and need some help with something at the cabin, Should take literally five minutes. Any way you can swing by my house after work this evening to help me take a look at a small box?"

Juan agrees, and they make plans for him to swing by around six.

## 38. *Investing in Eternity*

Joshua is doing some landscaping in the backyard when the alarm on his cell phone goes off. He looks at the screen to see Juan in his white work van heading up the driveway.

*Six p.m. sharp. I like this kid.*

Juan jumps out of the van and the two men shake hands.

"Joshua, hope you don't mind, but let's get to work. As soon as we are done here, I need to get back to the kitchen remodel I've been working on these past couple of days. I want to get it finished tonight and move onto another remodel job tomorrow."

"Of course," replies Joshua. "You certainly are a hard worker."

"Got to be. You know why I am trying to earn and save my money."

They both smile.

"So, what is this little box you need me to look at?"

Joshua takes a little blue box out of his pocket and hands it to Juan.

"Juan, I want you to have this."

Juan is speechless. He looks at the box for several seconds.

"Joshua, I can't take this ... It's too big of a gift ... Wow. What an honor for you to think of me. You barely know me ... Thank you ... But no."

"Don't be ridiculous, Juan. I bought this for the love of my life, thinking she would wear it all her life and that we would pass it on to our daughter or a daughter-in-law. But both my son and wife are gone. I've got no one to give it to. So please do me the honor of accepting my wife's wedding set. I have a good feeling about you and how much you are in love. I want the ring to have a good home where it will be appreciated and passed down for generations to come."

Juan opens the box to reveal a gold and titanium filigree wedding band and a matching diamond ring. It is a big and beautiful one, better than any diamond he has ever seen, and for sure a hundred times better than the "little stone in the corner" he had been hoping for.

His mouth falls open, lost in thought and overwhelmed with emotion. He looks up at Joshua. Both men have tears in their eyes.

"Enjoy it, Juan. It's yours now. God bless you and your marriage, and may you savor every moment you have together."

Juan eventually accepts, and Joshua encourages him to get going so he can finish his work for the day. Juan is glowing as he drives away from the cabin, joyful, hopeful. His mind is completely engrossed in planning the proposal and a humble wedding soon thereafter. Juan is perhaps the happiest man alive. Well, except for Joshua, that is, who is also glowing with joy as he relishes a love that still warms his heart.

## 39. Memphis

Joshua can't sleep. It isn't that sleeping on his mattress in the back of the Jeep is uncomfortable; he has slept in many worse places. It's that Joshua can't breathe. He has bronchitis, or perhaps pneumonia. He gets into the driver's seat, turns on the engine and heated seats, and starts looking up something from his phone.

*Perfect,* he thinks to himself. *I can be in Memphis in three hours.*

Joshua types the address into his GPS and drives away. Before he knows it, he is parked in front of a free medical clinic in down town Memphis. Although the sun just came up a few minutes earlier, Joshua is surprised to see so much traffic and activity. He parks the Jeep, making sure that the lock for his e-bike is fastened.

*Wouldn't want someone to steal my favorite toy, would we?*

After a few minutes in the waiting room, he is ushered by the assistant into Dr. Stephen Jefferson's office. It's a clean office, but has absolutely zero frills. And sadly, it still smells like the homeless man who just walked out.

"Dr. Jefferson, I am Joshua Stone. Thanks for seeing me so early this morning and thanks for being open."

Dr. Jefferson smiles. He is not used to having such a coherent patient so early in the morning. After explaining that he is having a hard time breathing and suspects bronchitis or pneumonia, the doctor gets to work checking out Joshua's vitals, heart, and lungs. Dr. Jefferson tells Joshua that most likely he has bronchitis. But without a chest x-ray, there is no way to know for sure. Since it is early and the x-ray tech has not yet arrived, Dr. Jefferson walks him into the next room and does the x-ray himself.

"So how did you end up here, Dr. Jefferson?"

"Well, I grew up not far from here. Went to school on a baseball scholarship. Played two years of 'pro' ball after graduating and then got hurt, a knee injury. So, I joined the Air Force and they paid for me to go to med school. I served for six more years then got out and came home to practice. A super handsome black guy with a medical degree is a good role model in these parts."

They both laugh.

"Okay, but why are you open so early? Why do you work for free?"

"Oh, nothing is free, Sir. Sunday, Monday, Tuesday I work here. And Wednesday, Thursday I work from my practice at the Baptist University Hospital. Two days of work there pay for three days of 'free' work here."

"You making any money?"

"No. I'm totally broke. Between the hospital administrators, the evil pharmaceutical companies, Medicare restrictions, paying my employees what they deserve, and malpractice insurance, I take home about four dollars an hour. At least it pays for my Mexican food addiction. Thankfully, I love what I do, so I don't need much more."

Joshua smiles. He really likes Dr. Jefferson.

Having noticed the espresso machine in Dr. Jefferson's office, Joshua shamelessly asks if he can have a cup of coffee before he leaves. Dr. Jefferson smiles and acquiesces.

Although Dr. Jefferson was being sarcastic about his good looks, he is quite handsome. With a big smile and a lean but athletic physique, he stands four inches taller than Joshua. *Doctors are always a bit too skinny,* thought Joshua. *Must be their emphasis on health. At least Dr. Jefferson likes coffee and Mexican food.*

"So, what's your story? You look and talk like you can afford health care. Why are you here?"

"I'm heading to visit a couple of friends on the East Coast and you were the closest doctor along my route. Thanks again for being open so early."

Joshua changes the subject. "Dr. Jefferson, you are a good man. What do you think the future of health care in America has in store for us? I would like to get your opinion."

They continue talking for a few more minutes. When their coffees are done, Jefferson gives Joshua a prescription for antibiotics.

"You should start taking these today, immediately after breakfast. The pharmacy across the street opens in an hour. Can you come back in ten days for a follow up?"

Joshua smiles, puts the prescription in his pocket, and thanks the doctor again for his help.

"You are a good man, Dr. Jefferson. I will be back through here in a week or ten days. It was a pleasure meeting you. In the meantime, I will pay your receptionist."

"Sorry, Joshua, everything here is free. You can make a donation online. But today, your health care was free."

"Thanks again, see you next week."

## 40. Harvard Law

Joshua is back in Professor Goldberg's office.

Already breathing better than he did three days earlier in Memphis, Joshua took the liberty of sleeping at a fancy hotel in Boston last night. After some clothes shopping, a hair and beard trim, his favorite orange chicken from the Pastry Factory, and a full night of sleep, Joshua is looking and feeling so much better.

In the waiting room, Joshua thinks to himself, *What a strange pair we are. Two men without justice. I am a man who has suffered such a stupid and pointless tragedy. One where justice really doesn't exist. And Skip Goldberg is a man who was denied justice by a judge who let a pedophile go free.*

"Joshua, please come in. How are you? You look great."

"I'm well, Professor, thanks for asking. I had bronchitis, but am on antibiotics. Don't worry. I am not contagious."

Joshua continues. "Thank you again for representing me in Tucson. The man who killed my family is a knucklehead, not a murderer. I just want him to do his time and get back to living his life. How was your time in Tucson? Did you play golf?"

"Eighteen holes at Saguaro Canyon, the most beautiful course in the world. Not to mention seeing my family. Thanks for kicking my butt and making me travel back home. It was good to be there.

"Listen, Joshua, I am so sorry about your loss. When you surprised me here last year, I didn't know your family just died. I am sorry. I trust that you are mourning appropriately and that each day gets a little easier."

"Don't worry about me, Professor. I'm suffering, for sure. But I am smart enough not to do anything dumb. Well, sort of …"

Joshua smiles. "I am working on a project and I need some legal advice. I started a company in Arizona. I bought a domain, but the website is not yet up and running. I know what the end state is, but I want to make sure that I do everything the right way so no one can argue it. Would you mind taking a look at this five-page 'Executive Summary' to make sure that it is legal and constitutional?"

"Constitutional? Um … okay. Of course, I will. I blocked you an hour, so let's at least get started now."

The professor takes seven minutes to scrutinize the "Executive Summary." Mesmerized, he puts the papers on his desk and looks around the room in a daze.

"I need some coffee!"

Joshua smiles. "Let's go. But my treat."

No one at the coffee shop, not in a million years, would have ever guessed the topic of discussion between the smiling law professor and his former student in the corner.

"Joshua, this is a great idea. But I need to think about it some more. It can work. I dare say it will work. But for sure you are going to need to do a few things. Off the top of my head, you are going to need to make sure that the leadership evaluation criteria is public from day one. That way no one is surprised by who wins. As long as it is written in the 'Terms or Conditions of Agreement,' which no one reads, then you are legally covered.

"Wow. Great idea. I hope you have some great computer programmers. This is going to get a lot of attention and be very complicated. Joshua … don't worry, I will keep my mouth shut. But we need to stay in touch. I need to think some more about this and put my ideas into writing."

"No problem, Skip. My contact info is at the end of the 'Executive Summary.' We will stay in touch. I am heading to the D.C. area later today to meet those computer programmers you just mentioned. But first, I am going to get some tacos at Jose's Taqueria."

"Oh, Joshua, Jose's is gone. It is now called Paco's Tacos. Same people, different name. Make sure you get some guacamole."

## 41. Cyber Command

The next day, Joshua and Mike walk through Cyber Command headquarters around lunchtime.

"Lunch time is the best," Mike explains to Joshua with his typical mischievous giggle. "This is where you get to see the true, awkward dynamic of the Cyber Command. In one corner of the cafeteria you see the managers. Guys like us in suits and ties. Alpha males, leaders, managers.

"In the far corner are the computer nerds. The guys who code and program. They have long hair, jeans, piercings, sit on the tables, have fun. Everyone in here has a top-secret clearance, and everyone here is a patriot. But it is the punk rockers versus the suits. Funny dynamic. Let's go talk with the guys I mentioned last night."

Mike introduces Joshua to the punk-rock corner as his boss in Afghanistan and all-over Latin America. The programmers nod in approval. It appears that Mike is the only "suit" who has broken down the imaginary barrier between the managers and the programmers. Joshua attributes this to the fact that while Michael had a bachelor's and master's degree, he was a Non-Commissioned Officer to his core. He could hang with the academics and officers, but always thought pragmatically and enjoyed the company of the guys who make it happen. He motions with his head to Robby and Rafael, and the four of them walk to the third corner of the cafeteria, totally empty.

Both in their late twenties, Robby and Rafael looked like two misfits. You would never have guessed by looking at them that they were so patriotic, or that their computer programming helped find and capture some of the most dangerous criminals walking the planet. Rafael looked like a flunky from a 1980s hair band. And Robby was wearing a scarf, a hoodie, a jacket, and a ski cap. He appeared ready for a walk above the Arctic Circle, not a private conversation in the corner of Cyber Command. After introductions, Joshua begins to explain his idea.

"Gentlemen, I want to start an online political party and get a Presidential Candidate and Vice President onto the ballot in all fifty states for next year's election. I want fifty million people to be able to become members of this political party. Let's simplify this and say they need to agree to our terms and conditions and then subscribe. I then want the subscribers to nominate leaders to compete for the Presidency and Vice Presidency. Nominations cost $1,000. This will keep out the riffraff. Those nominated will take a 100-question assessment. The winner gets the Presidential nomination and second place gets the Vice. What I need from you two gentlemen is to code the website. Make sure it is fast enough to handle the amount of traffic I know it is going to get. Then I want you to make a page where party members can nominate their bosses, leaders, professors, dads—whoever. Then the 100-question assessment gets emailed to them. I already have the 100 questions and the assessment weights for each question. Then I need a program to tally the answers from the candidates and let me know who the top two guys are. I don't want the business or website traceable to any of us, so we can maintain our privacy. What do you guys think? Can you do it?"

Robby and Rafael smile at each other then nod their heads up and down in agreement.

"We're in.  Let's do this."

Mike starts to giggle.

## 42. Church Service at the Doctor's Office

Back in Memphis, this time at Dr. Jefferson's office at Baptist University Hospital. Joshua is happy to see that his new doctor has such a plush office.

"Wow, great office. A little nicer than your other one."

Dr. Jefferson is glad to see Joshua again.

"Yes. As a hospital, the Baptists treat me really well. As a denomination, they are just as silly as all the other ones. Tell me, Joshua, do you go to church?"

"Yeah. Well, kind of," Joshua replies. "My brother Noah is starting a church online. He was sick and tired of the fact that the Bible says A but the church teaches B. The Bible says C, but the church does "D." So he started an online church. It's an unconventional church for unconventional people. He currently uploads devotional messages every day and a sermon every Friday… so the members can think about it during the Sabbath. Like Noah in the Bible, my brother Noah is a lone-ranger Christian working in a time when people are selfish and don't think about God. Although I support his church each month, everything he does is available for free. Kind of like you."

"Good to know. I'll check it out." Dr. Jefferson was sincere. "I've always felt the desire to honor God and to love my neighbor. I've simply reasoned that I can best do this by being a good doctor."

Dr. Jefferson gets back to business.

"Judging from today's x-ray, your bronchitis is gone. It looks like the antibiotics worked. Also, Mr. Stone, it looks like you gave my receptionist your insurance name: Milcare. So, you're former military, right?"

"Retired last year."

"Great, congratulations. What branch and service?"

"Army Special Forces."

"Cool. I thought so. Anyways, unlike your last visit, which was free, I will send a bill to Milcare for today's checkup."

They both smile.

"When will I see you next, Colonel Stone?"

"Lieutenant Colonel. But none of that, please. Call me Joshua."

"Okay. But only if you call me Stevie, like Stevie Wonder, just not as cool."

"We'll see each other in a little more than a year, Stevie. You need to save the dates next year for October ninth through the eleventh. I will contact you later with all the details. I promise. But I need your help for three days. I will pay for everything. I am working on a project and need your help. So please save those dates."

Dr. Jefferson agrees and makes a note in his calendar. He's a little confused, but not worried. Something about this patient gives him peace.

"I trust you," he says. "Looking forward to seeing what you have planned."

## 43. Campaign Manager

"Scary Larry" Whitfield smiles as Joshua enters the office. They shake hands.

"Joshua, good to see you. You look great."

"Thanks, Larry. Good to see you, too."

Joshua gets to business. "Listen Larry, I have a huge job for you and one which I know you can do well. This is going to change your life. I don't want to be melodramatic, but today everything changes. I'm starting a political party, and I want you to run it. I'm the boss and lead all policy decisions and content, but I am going to empower you to make it happen. Here is my proposal."

Joshua playfully slaps the latest version of his "America 1ˢᵗ Executive Summary" onto Larry's desk. A few minutes later, Larry looks up from reading it and smiles.

"I'm in. But I need a drink."

They both laugh.

"Do you have the money to make this happen?"

"Not really. I have $285,000 saved from selling my house in Tucson. But this is nothing next to the billion dollars that the Republicans and Democrats will have. We will have to do it on the cheap.

Larry begins the back brief: "Okay. So, you are starting a political party that's on the internet. Nominees pay a huge fee and then apply using a 100-question online assessment. The two winners are announced in October and the election is November third. I have to do all the background work to get a currently nonexistent political party onto the ballot in all fifty states, and besides that, campaign for a nameless and faceless President and Vice President who are finally revealed only one month before the election, using a campaign budget of a few hundred thousand dollars against the two major parties, which will have about a billion dollars each?"

Joshua nods.

"Okay. Let's do it," Larry announces confidently. "But first, I need a drink."

The two men walk out of the office, down a flight of stairs, and pop into the coffeeshop below.

"A large mocha Frappuccino, extra whip cream, please."

Joshua smiles. "Make that two."

## 44. Cabin Time

Joshua is happy to be back home. He throws his weekender on the floor, walks over to the kitchen, and pulls a Gewürztraminer out of the refrigerator. He is happy that everything is still working. He pours a glass of wine and sits on the couch, watching the sunset. He thinks of his wife and son. Every sunset reminds Joshua of them. He misses them so much. Tears begin to roll down his face. He doesn't wipe them away.

Taco appears out of nowhere and ends Joshua's pity party. He hisses violently at Joshua, enraged that Joshua deserted him for a few weeks. Fully grown, Taco looks like a minia-ture leopard: black, silent, elegant, but mean. Joshua is the only human who has touched him. Everyone else gets hisses and claws. When Joshua is away, Taco lives wild and hunts for his food. When Joshua is present, he enjoys leftovers.

During the next several weeks, Joshua tries to get into a rhythm. Going to bed early, getting up early, breakfast and an e-bike ride in the forest. Grocery shopping if needed. Afternoons are spent doing research and making coordinations. He speaks with Larry a few times a week, and with Robby and Rafael almost every day.

*We are at the point of no return.*

## 45. Election Day minus 12 Months (ED-12 months)

The "America 1st" Political Party goes live on November third. Joshua doesn't even turn his computer on that day. Instead, he goes for a long hike through the snowcapped mountains of Northern Arizona. It gets no media coverage, and only twenty people visit the website.

*Am I doomed to failure? No. I must continue as planned. I must drive on.*

## 46. Special Operations Command (SOCOM)

Thankfully, the weather is a bit warmer in Tampa Bay than the White Mountains of Northern Arizona. It's two weeks before Christmas when Sean Abbot greats Joshua at the SO-COM (Special Operations Command) visitor's center. Abbot, a tall, skinny, and scrappy-looking officer with small, frameless glasses, introduces himself and gives Joshua a strong handshake.

They walk through several hallways full of the bureaucrats who support the "Tip of the Spear," finally reaching Abbot's office. The sign on the door reads "Colonel Sean Abbot - Director of Finance, USSOCOM."

After being a very successful Medical Service Corps Officer, newly promoted Captain Sean Abbot was assigned to the SOCOM where he was in charge of the budget for medical equipment and supplies. Quickly realizing his ability to use money as a weapon system, the Special Operations Command sent him to get his MBA and DBA, and made him the Deputy Director of Finance. Fifteen years later, he still works in the same office. Staying in one place for fifteen years is unheard of in a community where officers change jobs every one to three years.

Joshua gets to business.

"Listen, Colonel Abbot. I know you are a very busy man and I am very thankful that your secretary has given me an hour of your time. I'm a former SF officer who retired about eighteen months ago.

"I want to ask you about money. How it works, how you get it, and how it flows? And what can you do in Washington D.C. to get more than your fair share of it? But first, I want to thank you, personally."

Abbot looks a bit confused.

"I've been deployed to Honduras twice in my career. During my second deployment, about ten years ago, I asked headquarters for a lot of money for 'Operation CENTURION SUNSET,' a simultaneous, multinational counter-narcotics operation throughout Central America. I only got about ten percent of the money I asked for, but it was more than enough to make a huge impact. So, thank you."

"Wait a second," interrupts Colonel Abbot with a smile, "CENTURION SUNSET was you! That was an amazing mission! Wow. Still can't believe that was you."

"It's an amazing story for another time," responds Joshua. "One I will gladly tell you over dinner or some good coffee. But I just wanted you to know that your efforts up here are even felt in the jungle … So, thanks again."

"My pleasure. Glad to have been a part of it. And for sure we need to stay in touch. I always wondered what happened."

Getting back on subject, Joshua continues to justify his visit: "Money is the single most important commodity in the Government. I want to own that subject and always be the smartest man in the room. But I have a lot to learn. I want to know about how money works at the highest levels. How does the U.S. annual budget work? The DOD (Department of Defense) budget work? The USSOCOM budget? How do the appropriation committees work?"

"Okay, so you want the forty-five-minute version of everything I have learned in the past twenty years."

"Absolutely. And then I am going to ask for a huge favor."

"Okay, Joshua. Thanks for being upfront. Let's start with the President's OMB, or Office of Management and Budget."

For the next two hours, Joshua soaks up everything Colonel Abbot tells him. He takes six pages of notes. It is clear that Abbot is a genius and that perhaps no one else in the Army better understands how the Government manages and budgets money. Sean tells a story of being asked the day after 9/11 how much would it cost to win the "Global War on Terror." A week later, the SOCOM staff came up with a dollar amount for the next five years. Realizing their inability to foresee and plan the requirements and actual costs of a new war against radical Islamists, Sean instinctively and single-handedly added another zero to the sum. Within a week, Congress appropriated the full request.

It is clear that despite Sean's grumpy disposition, he is a kind-hearted patriot, motivated to enable the fighting men of the Special Operations community with the best uniforms, weapons, equipment, tanks, trucks, and helicopters that money can buy.

Joshua ended their time together by asking for a job.

"Sean, I have six months to dedicate to learning all of this. But I don't want to go back to grad school. I want to see how it works in the real world. Where should I get a job? Where will I learn how our government handles money? I don't care where it is. I will even work for free. I just want to learn."

"That's easy. I have a good buddy who works in the OMB. I can get him to give you an internship. You won't earn anything, but you will learn everything."

Joshua leaves his contact info with Colonel Abbot and walks out of SOCOM headquarters without an escort.

*Time to get an apartment in DC,* thinks Joshua. *Sleeping in the Jeep is okay when travelling. But for six months in D.C., I need something fancier.*

## 47. National News Broadcast: America 1st Launches

Sitting in the Pancake House, Joshua looks up from his double-decker waffle to see his logo on the TV screen. He asks the waitress to turn the volume up.

"In other news, a still anonymous group of political activists have launched what they are calling 'America 1st' - a third political party which they predict will outperform the Republican and Democratic Parties in this year's election. They claim that only those capable of enduring the absurd campaign trail make it onto the ballot. These are not leaders to be respected and followed but political Machiavellians only capable of self-promotion."

"America 1st allows you, the people, to nominate leaders from anywhere in the country. Your boss, teacher, doctor, coach. Each nominee takes a 100-question test. The winners become the Presidential and Vice-Presidential candidate on the ballot this November."

"Although most scholars say this will certainly fail, many say that it is about time we use technology and the internet to find and support honest and legitimate leaders. Nonetheless, this initiative is gaining momentum. If this does turn out to be legitimate, we will continue to follow America 1st and their progress. Who knows, maybe it's time we put a leader, not another politician, back in the White House."

*I wonder if the President ever ate at the Pancake House. Probable not. Sad. His loss.*

## 48. The Victorian Fix-Me-Upper

Two miles from the White House, Joshua finds a room for rent in an old Victorian house inhabited by three law school students from Georgetown. One of their parents owns the place. The single-paned windows are oozing cold. The hardwood floors are anything but flat. The bathroom fixtures are fifty years old, and the shared appliances in the kitchen are twenty. This is clearly a rental property purchase that stretched the owners so far that they couldn't even make it livable for their son. It is a total Junker. Nonetheless, Joshua likes the Victorian charm, the location, his housemates, and the owners.

"I'll take it," declares Joshua. "But I have a favor. I only need the room through the last day of January. That makes thirteen months. Thirteen months of rent makes thirteen thousand dollars. Instead of paying rent, may I please upgrade the kitchen and my bathroom. Then when I move out, your son can move in."

The parents agree. After a quick discussion with Joshua regarding the quality of the intended upgrades, Joshua gives them $4,000 from his pocket.

"That's a $2,000 security deposit and $2,000 for my share of the water and electricity. If I owe you more, then please speak to me just before I move out."

Monday morning, a demolition crew from Brayden's Hardware arrives and busts out the old tiles, sink, toilet, and bathroom from Joshua's bathroom.

The next day, Joshua helps a plumber install a toilet, sink, and tub while the demolition crew busts out the kitchen.

Day three - The crew installs new cabinets while Joshua lays tile in his new bathroom.

Day four - The crew installs the sink and garbage disposal.

Day five - They install kitchen countertops and put double-pane windows in Joshua's bedroom.

And day six - They deliver the stainless-steel appliances.

It only takes a week, but the house looks five times better and everyone's quality of life significantly improves. Although all the upgrades will stay in the house, Joshua makes sure to remind his housemates that the new coffeemaker is his. When he leaves his room on the last day of January, he is going to take it with him to his new house. Everyone agrees.

## 49. The Intern

Joshua arrives at the White House's OMB at 0800 sharp, the first workday of March. He fills out paperwork and gets his access badge with two young interns and a senior accountant.

As it turns out, the two interns are best friends and roommates, straight out of John Hopkins University, in their early twenties: bright, eager, ambitious, and very pretty. Although Sarah and Amber look like junior business executives, they are sharing a room in a six-woman apartment, and together they have eighty-five dollars in their savings account.

The senior accountant, Rich Buchanan, is a full-time public servant, a GS15, who reminds the three interns at least half a dozen times that he is a GS15 and that he has been doing this for eighteen years. Although Joshua remains discreet, he inwardly giggles every time the self-righteous bureaucrat reminds them how awesome he is.

Everyone thinks that a forty-three-year-old intern with a short beard must be a joke, a spy, or an audit. Joshua gives his "elevator pitch" a hundred times that day: "I'm just here for a six-month internship. I have a great job lined up for January. But between now and then, I thought it would be a good idea to learn a bit more about how the government uses money. So literally, I'm just here to learn and observe. Please let me know how I can help you out."

Of course, the director of the OMB accepted Joshua's internship as a personal favor to COL Sean Abbot. But no one else knew of this arrangement. They only saw a forty-three-year-old intern.

*How unconventional.*

The interns are assigned work in three different offices. They will do a two-month rotation in each office. Sarah will start in the "Policy Office," Amber in "Management," and Joshua will work directly for Rich Buchanan in "Budget."

*Super,* thinks Joshua. *Not looking forward to working for that idiot.*

Upon learning that Joshua will be his intern, Richard Buchanan asks if he will help him carry a box of office supplies from his car into his new office. Of course, Joshua nods in agreement.

They walk to the parking lot, where Richard pulls a heavy box of books from the back seat of his filthy and cluttered Mazda coupe and hands it to Joshua. Richard grabs his briefcase and an umbrella and the two men walk back to the office.

Once back in the office, Richard asks Joshua to unpack the books onto the shelf behind his desk. When Joshua finishes, Buchanan asks for a cup of coffee.

"Great idea, Richard. I'll go scout out the coffee options here in the office and bring back the best one. Do you take cream or sugar?"

"I didn't spend eighteen years becoming a GS15 so that my interns can call me by my first name. Call me Mr. Buchanan or Sir. I drink my coffee black. So, go steal me a cup wherever you can and hurry back, you have a lot of work to do today."

### 50. Going for a Swim

It is Sunday evening and Joshua is relaxing on a park bench, enjoying the sunset across the Potomac. The oranges and blues fill the sky.

*D.C. certainly has its moments.*

After a week of being treated like trash from a lazy and arrogant bureaucrat, Joshua is glad to have a few minutes of silence to relax and think.

His peace is interrupted by a distant scream. It is a young woman. She is running along the river about 100 meters upstream. It looks like someone has fallen into the Potomac and is drifting in his direction.

Joshua runs to the riverbank to get a better look, seeing dimly a flailing kid drifting in the aggressive current.

*Oh, please. No! Not now. How could someone be so stupid that they fall into the river?*

Joshua instinctively starts ripping of his clothes. As he is doing so, his brain rapidly conducts some risk analysis and consequence management:

*It's cold as ice in the water. Stupid kid has about a minute, but I'd give myself three. I should just let him die. It would serve him right for falling in. Idiot. What would happen to America 1ˢᵗ without me? What is the greater good? America 1ˢᵗ or a stupid kid? No! Think of the parents. All life is precious. I've got to try.*

*Great, there is a dock 200 meters down river. Not sure I can grab the kid and swim over before the current sweeps us away.*

*Ahhhhh! Let's do it. Help me, God.*

Now in his underwear, Joshua tracks the kid, waiting for the right moment, then jumps into the Potomac and swims to him. The boy is blue and barely moving. Joshua cradles him under his left arm, and with his right arm and legs begins to side-stroke back to shore.

*Wow, this water is colder than I thought,* thinks Joshua. *I'm getting too old for this."*

Joshua keeps swimming for all he's worth. It takes about ninety seconds to reach a small dock along the river bank. Joshua is exhausted like he just ran a marathon. The hysterical mother arrives with a half-dozen bystanders. They pull the kid onto dry land and wrap him in jackets to help raise his body temperature. Frozen solid, Joshua slowly pulls himself onto the dock and stands up.

*I must be exhausted. Climbing three steps up a ladder was never so difficult.*

A minute later, the paramedics arrive. Joshua gives them a quick back brief as they smother the kid with wool blankets and begin treating him for shock.

Joshua assesses his situation and starts laughing out loud. *Five minutes ago, everything was great. And now I'm standing in the middle of Washington D.C., soaking wet, frozen solid, wearing one sock, one shoe, and my underwear. I'm such an idiot.*

Joshua starts jogging up river, partially to stay warm and partially to get away from all the people. A minute later, he is at his bike. Thankfully, it was not stolen. Joshua gets dressed but can't find his other shoe. It must have fallen into the water.

*I will have to write that shoe off in my taxes,* thinks Joshua as he begins to pedal off.

Just then he is stopped by a young man running behind him.

"Wait," the man yells. "Who are you? Why did you do that? You're a hero. Don't run away. We need to be able to thank you. You saved that kid's life."

Joshua stops and looks the man in the face.

"When I was young and tough, I used to be a Special Forces Combat Diver. We swam in water colder than that a hundred times. I'm only thankful that I was in the wrong place at the right time. Now, please, let me get home and dry off. I don't want or need any publicity right now. I just did the right thing."

With that, the one-shoed man rides home, takes a quick shower, and rushes into town to buy some new wingtips.

## 51. National News: The Cinderella Shoe

During a coffee break in the OMB, Joshua finds his new colleagues glued to the television. The news is reporting the story of a Down syndrome kid who fell into the Potomac River yesterday evening.

"An anonymous man jumped in and rescued the kid. The hero refused to identify himself but did say that he was a former Special Forces SCUBA Diver and that he didn't want any publicity. The primary witness to the situation says that the hero rode off on a bike with only one shoe. The paramedic crew found a black wingtip floating at the dock where the boy was rescued. Inside the shoe, under a foam insert, was a 100-dollar bill and a stainless-steel saw blade. Perhaps this man really was Special Forces. Anyone who has information about this shoeless hero should please contact our broadcast company. We want to give him a proper reward ... and of course, buy him a new pair of shoes."

Joshua turns and walked away. Halfway down the hall he could still hear the broadcast ...

"In other news, the America 1ˢᵗ political party is gaining momentum, with over one million members. Still, no one knows who is backing this party with money and ideology. Even the U.S. Government can't find the source code of this website. Nonetheless, they have enough signed petitions to get their candidate on the ballot in eight states, with more states joining every week. Will it be enough? Skeptics say no."

Joshua smiles as he walks back his desk. His new shoes fit perfectly.

## 52. *Learning How the Government Doesn't Budget*

The next two months pass slowly. This is mainly because Joshua's new boss, Rich Buchanan, is living up to his first impression.

Upon realizing how talented Joshua is, Buchanan keeps giving him more and more work to do. Joshua doesn't really mind. After all, he was there to learn the business.

The world of governmental finances was very complicated and very discouraging. What was most discouraging was the fact that Buchanan was a tyrant. He never said thank-you, and he took all the credit for Joshua's projects as if they were his own work. He was exactly opposite to how a public servant ought to be.

In order to maintain his anonymity, Joshua did the best he could to be the gray man. To blend in. To be unnoticed. Although Superman was about to come out of the closet, he was playing the part of Clark Kent as best he could.

Nonetheless, it was impossible to remain anonymous. Although he avoided eye contact and always kept to himself, everyone at the OMB liked Joshua. He was the fatherly figure who always gave good advice. He was the humble man who volunteered for every thankless job. He was the man who rode his e-bike to work. He was the man who always did the dishes and took out the trash, both at the office and at his house.

At the end of the two months working for Buchanan, Joshua feared how Sarah or Amber would react to his harsh and unjust leadership.

*I'm going to have to keep an eye on that guy. I just don't like or trust him.*


## 53. Getting Stronger

Back at "Headquarters" in Jackson Hole, Wyoming, Scary Larry is doing the best he can to ensure that the America 1ˢᵗ political party is proceeding as planned.

The organizational model is quite simple: Larry is the mastermind for the election process. He works day and night by himself from his office at his law firm, above the coffee shop. Everything is decided, communicated, monitored, and delegated online. People volunteer via the website. Volunteers are organized by states and city. Each state has a state lead in the capital city. That person is the interface with the state legislature to ensure that they are following the protocol to get a candidate properly written onto the Presidential ballot in that state. Monday mornings, the "cities" have an online meeting with the "state" team. Monday afternoons, the "states" have an online meeting with the "region" team. And Tuesday mornings, the "regions" have their online meeting with "Headquarters."

Presidential candidate nominations are beginning to flow in. Robby and Rafael are in charge of this part of the process. Once a candidate is nominated, terms of agreement are accepted, and the $1,000 "nomination" payment is confirmed, the candidate is sent a questionnaire. Only Robby and Rafael have access to the graded results. The Presidential and Vice-

Presidential candidates will be announced in October, one month before elections.

Now that "A1" has some money trickling in, Larry has agreed that each state team is authorized one small office. Each state office has the exact same layout, using identical Ikea couches and tables. Although most A1 voters are signing up online, many are stopping by these state offices to sign the petition to put the A1 candidates on the election ballet. While there, they can pick up a flier or sticker, learn more, register as a volunteer, and, of course, make a donation. None of the volunteers are paid. Headquarters covers rent, electricity and printing. State leads are given a laptop to ensure the security of the names of the A1 supporters.

"If Thomas Jefferson didn't need a hundred-million-dollar champagne budget, then we don't either," Larry keeps explaining. "Grassroots political efforts require only passion and commitment. If we can successfully accomplish with thousands of dollars what the Democrats and Republicans do with hundreds of millions, then we are one step closer to demonstrating to American voters that we are the solution to our collective political and leadership problems."

Larry and Joshua agree that it is time to hire a press secretary. Joshua recommends interviewing a hometown journalist and emerging YouTube "vlogger" who has been focusing on "good news" stories. After watching her heart breaking, but informative, three-part document series on single mothers raising children after their husbands were killed in Iraq, Joshua and Larry, both in tears, agreed she would be the perfect addition to the team. Larry sets up an interview, and a week later Priscilla Kartoff walks into Headquarters to begin work.

After a morning cappuccino, Priscilla shows Larry her communications plan for the next few months, her plan to reveal the Presidential and Vice-Presidential candidates a month before the election, and her communications plan during the final days before the election. After a few hours of discussion and just a little refining, they call Joshua to get a final approval. He agrees.

Without even a desk or a phone, living in a hotel room, and exhausted by a two-day drive, Priscilla earned her weight in gold within hours of joining the team. Joshua and Larry could not be happier with her brilliant plan.

A classic millennial girl, Priscilla was always a genius at marketing, social media, and communications. Even as a penniless college student, her Instagram looked like a Hollywood diva's. She was on the rise as a prominent newscaster when a local tragedy caused her to rethink her career goals. She then decided she would focus on being a positive and uplifting journalist, a story-teller. Although she never shies away from telling the truth, her preference is to focus on stories which educate, inspire, and strengthen.

Priscilla's European ancestry endowed her with a tall, skinny frame, strong cheekbones, full lips, light brown eyes, and long, straight brown hair, which she curled earlier that morning in her long-term hotel room in Jackson Hole. Even as a teenager, everyone she met immediately thought she just walked off the cover of a European fashion magazine. Although today she is one of the most beautiful women in America, she doesn't get dressed up for Joshua or Larry, but for herself, out of integrity and self-respect. She has discovered that her outward beauty is only a reflection of her inward character and professional competence. Priscilla is a welcomed addition to the America 1st team.

## 54. Getting Burned

Priscilla's second day of the work is not as joyful as her first.

Upon arriving just after dawn to her new office, she is met by a half-dozen police cars and fire trucks. She parks and begins looking for Larry.

The office is destroyed. Burnt. The brick walls are covered in black charcoal and smoke. Although it's only her second day on the job, she believed in the job. She is fully committed to the idea of Americans electing a leader who is not a politician. She starts to cry.

"Another good idea destroyed by the hands of the evil political machine," she whispers quietly to herself.

Tears are running down her face as she desperately looks for Larry. She asks the first policeman she runs into if anyone was hurt.

He assures her that no one was hurt.

Relieved that Larry was not in the building, she instinctively takes out her cell phone and begins filming.

Minutes later, Larry finishes making his statement to the police and walks out of their make-shift command center in the next-door office. He finds Priscilla documenting the fire, smoky tears still on her face, and pulls her aside to reassures her. "No one was hurt. So that is good news."

He moves in closer and lowers his voice. "But better yet is the fact that Joshua made me set up a full security system last month. Everything was recorded. Robby and Rafael are looking at the footage now, and we have a conference call with Joshua, Robby and Rafael, and Skip, our lawyer, in an hour. Let's see what else we can learn between now and then."

A few minutes later, the firemen confirm that the structure is safe and that Larry and Priscilla are allowed upstairs. It only takes a minute to confirm Larry's suspicion.

"My laptop is not on my desk. They stole it," Larry says out loud. "This was sabotage. And now that they have my laptop, we know who they are and where they are."

Priscilla nods, ready for action. "They messed with the wrong team."

## 55. Washington Memorial

At precisely 0800 Washington D.C. time, Joshua begins the video teleconference with the entire America 1st team from his tablet. Wearing a dress shirt and tie, you can see the Washington Memorial in the background. It is a beautiful day, and Joshua is taking a morning stroll through the mall before heading into his internship.

Upon seeing Joshua for the first time, Priscilla's face goes white, then completely flushed. She takes a deep breath to keep herself from passing out. She can't believe it.

*"I know that guy,"* she thinks to herself. *"That was the guy whose family died in a car accident when I was working for the local news in Tucson.*

*"I'll never forget how he yelled at us. I felt like such a bad person. The reason I quit that job was because of him, because of that story."*

*"I can't believe he hired me. Even after I ran the story about his family getting killed. And now..."*

Priscilla snaps out of her thoughts and rejoins the video teleconference.

"Larry and Priscilla, where are you right now and do you feel safe? Are you safe?"

"Both," Larry replies.

Priscilla, still a bit flushed, is glad for once that someone else is doing the talking.

"We feel safe and are safe." Larry continues. "We're actually at my house. Looks like they got what they were after, the computer. We should be safe for now."

"Good to hear that you are both safe. Priscilla just started working yesterday. She hasn't had time yet to do all of our security training … So please teach her what you can and Robby and Rafael will express-mail your new laptops to you later today."

"So now it is over to you, Robby and Rafael. What do we got?"

"What we got is a freaking gold mine," explodes Rafael. "We have security camera footage of two guys pulling into the parking lot behind the building. I knew those idiots would park there. It was the obvious choice. We have footage of them breaking in the door, ransacking the office, taking the laptop, and lighting a fire with a candle to make it look like a mistake."

"Both of the guys are big and scary. One looks like a glamour boy with perfect combed salt-and-pepper hair, and the other has an awesome rockabilly mustache with waxed tips."

"Best yet, they turned on the computer about twenty minutes ago to copy the hard drive. We now know what they look like and who these glamour criminals are. All you have to do is say the word, Joshua, and we will execute the virus they just downloaded."

"Whoa whoa whoa," interrupts Skip Goldberg, already in a sweater and tie, drinking a cup of coffee from his kitchen. "What virus are you talking about?"

"Thanks, Rafael, I'll take it from here," Joshua responds. "We always suspected that the Republican or Democratic National Committees might try to sabotage our operation."

"The Dems are the worse," interjects Rafael. "We're always having problems with them at Cyber Command."

"That's enough, Rafael," continues Joshua. "Unfortunately, we all know that the threat is real and that people in power do terrible things to maintain it. We knew the biggest threat would be to Scary Larry's office …"

Larry interrupts, "Not sure who this 'Scary Larry' character is. Perhaps you can call him 'Loving Larry.'"

Everyone laughs.

Joshua continues, "As I just said, we knew the biggest threat would be at the A1 Headquarters. So, we rigged up a super security system and even placed cameras on adjacent parking lots. More importantly, we set the security on our laptops so that when someone turns on the computer but doesn't go through our security process, the laptop's camera records and posts video to our database. Everything they have access to on the laptop is false, and is encoded with our blockchain security code. We can use it as we want … But I recommend we track where this blockchain goes and keep it available in case we need to use it later."

"What do you mean, 'use it later'?" questions Skip.

Robby takes it from there. "Let's assume that our laptop makes its way back to the FBI. It makes sense that the U.S. Government wants to ensure that this emerging political party is not being backed by Islamic radicals or Russian capitalists. We would expect the government to spy on our activities. If this is the case, we accept the vandalism and let the insurance pay the bill.

"But this is not the case because the FBI doesn't set fires. They simply would have stolen the computer or copied it. So, this is clearly an act of desperation by someone threatened by the momentum we are making. If we track this to the lead Democratic or Republican candidate, then we could post the videos and circumstantial evidence on the internet right before the election. We can fight their evil with our truth. They will have to drop out of the race and we will win all of their voters.

"More likely is that they take us to court for being unconstitutional. Perhaps we can use this evidence to convince them to drop the charges.

"And of course, the Boy Scout solution is to turn all this evidence over to the police and let the Jackson Hole Police Department, cowboy boots and all, see the videos, make the association with the national political candidates, and make arrests as appropriate.

"Either way, we gained a huge upper hand in this chess game, and all it cost me was a few internet cameras and a laptop. What do you think, Skip?"

"I used to think that Joshua was paranoid," replies Skip. "But now I think he was appropriately paranoid. I agree. No way this is the FBI. It has to be a rogue candidate. I prefer the Boy Scout method where we turn over all the evidence to the local police. But let's see where these blockchains take us and make our decision later in the week. In the meantime, I want to do some research on our right to publicly release security camera and laptop images. I don't think that even the Supreme Court would disagree with the fact that a person or business is allowed to upload to YouTube videos taken from their own security cameras and stolen laptops. But let me look into it."

## 56. National News: America 1ˢᵀ Headquarters Mysteriously Burns Down

"The America 1ˢᵗ political party has suffered another defeat. This one is of their own doing. Sources in Jackson Hole, Wyoming, home of the America 1ˢᵗ national headquarters, have confirmed that a candle left unattended in the office started a fire late last night, burning the entire building, including the coffeeshop downstairs. No one was injured in the event. Looks like this pipedream of a political movement has gone up in smoke."

## 57. Dinner Guests

Later that evening, BG John Morrison knocks on the door of Joshua's D.C. house in a total uproar. Mike Campos is already there.

Joshua pours three glasses of red wine then puts the steaks on the grill.

"Great wine," Morrison begins. "Thanks. All in all, Joshua, you look healthy and your eyes aren't as sad as they were last year. But don't let yourself get fat."

"John. Always glad to spend some time with you. Honest to a fault. I'm doing as well as I can. And don't worry, I won't let myself get fat."

They all smile.

"Mike," continues Morrison, "nothing to say about you. You always look terrible. You walk funny. It's a miracle you're still alive. Hasn't that pretty wife of yours taught you any-thing about moisturizers, tucking in your shirt, or God forbid combing your hair?"

"At least I still have hair, Your Royal Highness," retorts Mike without a second's hesitation.

Morrison changes the subject. "Mike said you were up to something but wouldn't tell me what it is. I know you'll tell me when the time is right. Right?"

Joshua replies, "Yes, Sir. I'm up to some major shenanigans. But I don't want you involved. At least not yet. But don't worry. Everything is legal. We even have a lawyer at Har-vard keeping me on track."

The three friends enjoy telling war stories and catching up.

Mike talks about his boys and how they surprisingly love life up here in the D.C. area. Joshua tells Morrison about all that he did to fix up the cabin and how Mike made him buy two $4,000 e-bikes. And John tells them about calling the Chair-man of the Joint Chiefs a dinosaur. They ask for the details.

"You know, guys, a young Special Forces Officer speaks Ar-abic, uses night-vision goggles, has thermal optics and scopes on his rifle, blends in with the people, communicates securely via unconventional and conventional methods, has a master's degree from a reputable university, and has spent half his career in combat in a third-world country.

"A senior General speaks only English, spent the first twenty years of his career planning to fight tank battles against east-ern European nations, which are now our NATO allies. His career highlights were training rotations in the desert of Cal-ifornia and his first combat tour was from a headquarters when he was fifty years old. He is a dinosaur. No wonder the United States wins every battle but has lost every war since Vietnam.

"I'm sure I am going to get fired now. Or sent to Africa. Either way, I don't have the patience to deal with all these bureaucrats. They're so wishy-washy. They have no vision, no direction, no momentum. We deserve better leaders. Even as a Brigadier, I am not satisfied with my peers and seniors."

Mike jumps into the conversation: "I agree. My peers are terrible. Either they are jerks, or incompetent, or lazy. To be fair, they usually aren't all three. But for sure, I never run into anyone these days who is competent, hardworking, and a good dude. Aren't there any worthy leaders these days?"

"I think so," responds Joshua. "But for the most part, the world is led by politicians, not leaders. Men who love to campaign and use social media and hear themselves talk. These clowns aren't worthy of our loyalty. That is why we need to step up one day. If not us, who?"

General Morrison interjects, "If not us, who. Put a sock in it, Joshua. Are you stupid? We've given our best years and strength to our country. And what did it give back? Josh, the second you got out of the Army to focus on being a good husband and father, everything was stolen from you. No idea what you have planned, but from what I see, you're working for free as a stupid intern for a bunch of idiots who can't balance a budget. Mike spent half his life in third-world countries, he walks like a 100-year-old lady, and how does the military repay him? They make him leave the best job in the military to work for a bunch of ungrateful and unworthy misfits up here in D.C. As for me … all the government has given me is pain, suffering, deployments, injuries, and two Purple Hearts. Screw service. I can't wait to retire, mind my own business, and ski every day till my knees give out."

Realizing that he is preaching to the choir, John tries to calm himself. "Speaking of retirement, we kicked the renters out of our condo and plan to move to Vail in a couple months.

You guys are always invited. Mike, please bring Maria and the boys, too."

"John, you talk a big game," retorts Mike. "But service is in your blood. You don't know anything else and wouldn't be happy doing anything else. Even after telling the chairman that he is a dinosaur, if you were offered a good job, you would take it."

"No way. You could offer me the moon and I would turn it down. I'm done serving my country. It doesn't deserve my service."

Joshua and Mike exchange smiles. Mike, of course, lets out a ridiculous giggle. Joshua concludes the conversation: "I guess we'll see about that when the time comes."

## 58. Lincoln Memorial

Joshua's two-month internship in the OMB Policy Office has come to an end. Everyone from the director to the janitor knows Joshua, and they are sad that he is leaving. Although there is a quietness and a sadness about Joshua, his integrity, humility, and hard work are contagious. His colleagues throw a surprise picnic for him on the steps of the Lincoln Memorial, catered by his favorite Mexican food restaurant.

The day is warm and the sun is glorious. Having spent four months in Washington, Joshua is still captivated by its beautiful monuments and skylines.

*I wish Colette and Jacob were here. I still miss them so much. This crazy plan of mine would be so much more bearable and happier if they were at my side.*

Halfway through the lunch, Joshua stands up to thank his colleagues and new friends for the picnic. He also humbly reminds them that while budget policy is not the most exciting thing he ever did in his life, he was glad to have had the opportunity to learn so much and to enjoy such a remarkable experience.

After finishing his last taco, Joshua grabs his sweet tea and walks over to Sarah and Amber to ask how they are doing.

Amber begins immediately: "I hate that jerk Buchanan. What a pig. I am so glad that I am done working for him. Management was wonderful. Budget was miserable. I just hope the policy team likes me as much as they liked you guys."

Sarah continues: "I'm actually a bit afraid for the next two months. I had the two good jobs, and Monday I start my rotation with the jerk. Promise me you guys come by regularly to help me out and to check in on me."

"Okay. We promise."

## 59. National News: Democratic Presidential Candidates Johnson-Kennedy

"After a bloody and undignified primary election, emotions were high last night at the Democratic National Convention where former President Barack Obama was present to announce the Democratic Presidential ticket. Former Congressman Mark Riley was beat out by the strong and charismatic team of Senator Johnson from California and his running mate Rose Kennedy of Massachusetts."

Senator Johnson: "I've served as a senator for the past eleven years, focusing on bringing more jobs and more social programs to the great state of California. It is now my pleasure to focus on bringing jobs and social programs to the rest of the nation. Vice President Rose Kennedy and I will close the gap between the haves and have-nots. Equality for all!"

Although there were dozens of contentious themes debated during the primary elections, all candidates from the Democratic Party unanimously agree that there is absolutely no threat from the America 1st political party. There is no way that an unknown outsider could steal victory this election."

## 60.  Getting Fired

The fifth month of Joshua's internship flies by. Joshua is enjoying learning about how to manage the nation's money.

He takes a coffee break and decides to swing by Buchanan's office to check on Sarah. She seems to be preoccupied these days, and his fatherly instinct is kicking in.

As Joshua nears Buchanan's office, he hears an argument within: "Stop it, Sir. I already told you that's not appropriate."

"Come on, Sarah. You little flirt. I know you want it."

"Stop it, Sir. I mean it. Leave me alone …"

Joshua pushes the door open to see Buchanan assaulting Sarah in the corner of his office. He is attempting to smother her with kisses while using his body and arms to prevent her from pushing away. One of his hands is trying to grab her butt. Sarah is trying to resist, but Buchanan is much bigger and stronger.

"What the hell are you doing in here! Leave at once. Sarah and I are just having an argument. It is none of your business. Leave immediately."

Ignoring Buchanan, Joshua sees the fear in Sarah's eyes and tells her to leave. She breaks away from Buchanan's grip and heads for the door.

"Sarah," Joshua continues is a calm and calculated voice, "please go get security and call for a medic. Mr. Buchanan has been hurt and needs immediate medical care."

Joshua shuts the door behind Sarah as she walks out to do as she was told.

Joshua slowly approaches Buchanan, "So, you like forcing yourself on little intern girls? Shame on you. How come bullies like you never pick on someone your own size?"

Buchanan starts cussing at Joshua and pointing at his face. "Mind your own business, intern boy. You walk out of this office right now or you're done." He aggressively thumps Joshua in his chest.

*That's it.*

Joshua grabs Buchanan's finger like a vise, instantaneously pivoting 180 degrees while rotating his grip. Buchanan flips to the ground and screams in pain. Joshua kicks Buchanan's elbow, shattering it to pieces. He then grabs the rest of Buchanan's fingers and breaks all of them backwards. Buchanan screams again and starts rolling around on the ground in agony. He eventually passes out from the pain.

A minute or two later, the security officer arrives. Joshua explains the situation from his perspective and they call an ambulance.

Mr. Buchanan regains consciousness as the paramedics arrive. As they escort him out of the office and to the ambulance, everyone in the building could hear him screaming: "You're done, Joshua, intern boy. Hope you have a good lawyer. You don't know who you are messing with. You'll will never work in this city again. You're done. I'm going to ruin you."

## 61. National News: Democratic National Party Sues

"With the election less than four months away, the "America 1st" Party is being challenged in our nation's highest court. Both the Democratic and Republican National Party concur that America 1st is unconstitutional. The court will hear both arguments September 23rd."

## 62. Campaign Headquarters

Despite protecting Sarah from sexual assault and only hurting Rich Buchanan after he violated Joshua's personal space by thumping his chest, Joshua was asked to leave the OMB while they investigate the incident.

Joshua takes a few more days in D.C. to settle bills, out-process the OMB, turn in his access badge, and have one last dinner with Mike Campos and his family.

He packs up the jeep and heads west. Three days later he is back in Jackson Hole to take care of another emerging problem.

"I'm pulling up now," Joshua tells Larry as he enters the parking lot of the strip mall where the new campaign headquarters has been located for the past few months.

"Okay, I see it. The black Suburban in the back of the parking lot. Are you sure that's the one?"

"Of course, we're sure," Larry replies. "They've been here off and on all week."

"I'm going to keep my phone on and in my pocket. Try to record this conversation on your end. I'm heading in to investigate."

Joshua approaches the Suburban from the side, stopping about twenty feet from the passenger-side doors. He puts his Jeep in park, keeps the lights on, and walks up to the back seat and knocks on the tinted window.

"Can I help you gentlemen?"

After knocking a second time, all the doors open at once and four of the biggest men Joshua has ever seen get out.

*Oh, no. Not this. I got no back up and these dudes are big,* thinks Joshua as he tries to calmly assess the situation. He repeats the question: "Can I help you gentlemen?"

"You work for America 1ˢᵗ, right? Who is the boss? We want to talk to him." The four goons start to encircle Joshua.

Although the Jeep's headlights are on, their light creates long shadows, making it hard for Joshua to see what the men look like. About the same time that he recognizes the man with the rockabilly moustache, he sees that all of them are wearing gloves. *These guys aren't here to volunteer,* thinks Joshua.

"Nice gloves. You guys look like a bunch of thugs. I doubt you want to have a conversation with anyone. What do you really want?"

The first guy attacks from the left. Joshua parries his punch, and counters with a ridge hand to the throat and a knee to the stomach. He grabs the man's head with both hands and drops to the ground, taking the man with him. His head hits the asphalt so hard that he's instantly unconscious. Within a blink, Joshua springs back to his feet and faces his second attacker.

A second attacker moves in but hesitates when Joshua throws a deceptive front hand jab. Joshua sweeps his attacker's front leg and almost instantly follows up with a round kick to his head. The mustache man hits the ground hard. He will be in-capacitated for several seconds, but is not yet unconscious and out of the fight.

Feeling a pinch in his left hamstring, Joshua realizes he has just been tasered. It's too late. He falls to the ground. Within seconds, the remaining two thugs are punching and kicking Joshua repeatedly. He curls into the fetal position, trying to protect his face and head. After a few dozen blows, the mustache man is back on his feet and comes over to kick Joshua while he is down. Eventually, the assaulters relent.

Half-conscious and in a lot of pain, Joshua rolls onto his back, thankful the kicks have stopped. He focuses on breathing.

The mustache man signals the other two to put their still unconscious colleague in the Suburban. He then kneels down over Joshua's head.

"You awake, dude?"

"Can you hear me?"

"I got a message for you to pass on to your boss. Can you remember it?"

Joshua nods up and down, barely able to see through his bloody and swollen eyes.

"We're not too happy with you and your stupid political party. Drop out of the race this week, or we are going to burn down all of the campaign offices … And this time we aren't going to wait till the middle of the night when no one is there. You hear me? You have till Friday or there will be innocent blood. And it will be all your fault. Do you understand me?"

Joshua takes a few deep breaths, preparing to answer. He signals the man closer. "I've seen adolescent boys with better mustaches."

With that, the mustache man picks up Joshua's head by the hair and gives him one last punch to the face.

Joshua passes out.

## 63. Trauma Center

Thankfully, the Jackson Hole hospital is used to multi-traumas, as it caters to skiers and snowboarders who take nasty falls down the mountain. Trauma is normal, but "assault and battery" were very much the exception.

Larry and Priscilla are in the room when Joshua wakes up. He's been knocked out for about eight hours. Priscilla is in tears, an emotional wreck. After a few minutes of small talk, Joshua falls back to sleep for several more hours.

When Joshua finally wakes up, he is surprised to see Mike sitting in a chair next to him.

"Looks like sleeping beauty is waking up," Mike begins, this time without the giggle. He leans closer to Joshua with the cocky smile that men who have seen war together share when times are hard.

"Hey, brother, just like the old times."

Genuinely glad to see Mike, Joshua lets out a small smile. Within a few more minutes and he regains his mental focus and starts asking coherent questions. Larry's been at the hospital the longest so he starts the back brief.

"You can't see well yet because your right eye is swollen shut and your left one is not much better. But no permanent damage. The swelling should go down in a few days. They did an MRI on your head. Everything checks out. Six broken ribs. Your nose was broken. It was sideways when the ambulance arrived. The ER doc set it while you were knocked out. You right ear was torn; eighteen stitches. Doctor says that although you look like a freak of nature right now, you will look like a human again in a few weeks."

"Are you two okay?" asks Joshua. "Did anything happen to you?"

This time Priscilla speaks up: "We're good, Joshua. That's kind of you to ask. We're just scared and shaken up. It all happened so fast. We felt so helpless. After calling the police, we rushed down to check on you. It seemed like an eternity before the ambulance arrived. You were lying there all bloody. It was terrible."

"What about my dash cam?" asks Joshua. "Did it work?"

"Don't know yet," replies Larry. "I stuck the memory card in my laptop and Robby and Rafael are looking at it as we speak."

"I'm not in any pain. Can I go home?"

"No way," Mike chuckles. "Seriously, Joshua. Aren't you paying attention? You're messed up and should be thankful to be alive. You don't feel any pain because you are on some bigtime drugs right now. Doctor's says that no matter what, you're staying here at least a week for observation and pain management."

## 64. Crisis Management

Six days later Joshua pulls into the driveway of his cabin. Exhausted from the drive, he opens the patio window for some fresh air and crashes onto the couch. Joshua wakes up a few hours later to a cat hissing. It's Taco, standing on Joshua's chest, rebuking him for being away for so long.

*Yeah, yeah. yeah. Join the club. Everyone hates me.*

Joshua opens a can of cat food from the pantry, swallows down another pain pill, and returns to the couch for nine more hours of sleep.

The next morning, Joshua has a video teleconference with the entire A1 team. Everyone is in a panic. They look great but are acting like the sky is falling. Joshua looks like a prisoner of war but is at total peace.

*Looks are always so deceiving.*

Joshua attempts to calm everyone down, but even he knows the facts in the back of their heads... he was just fired from his internship, beat up almost to the point of death, and the A1 political party is being sued for being unconstitutional by the Democratic National Committee and has a Supreme Court date in six weeks.

Joshua can do nothing more than reassure his team that their quest is noble and that they have a good plan and should see it through to execution. He hopes they believe him.

Larry brings up the fact that they have to address one final question: What to do with the video evidence of the two men burning down the campaign headquarters and the four men beating up Joshua?

Skip interrupts: "There is nothing to discuss. We will remain dignified and take the Boy Scout approach. After I win in the Supreme Court, which I will, Larry will turn over all the video evidence to the local Jackson Hole police. They're not corrupt. So, for sure they are going to make arrests. Once the press gets ahold of this story, it will spin out of control ... all in our favor. Man! They brought this on themselves. So sad that our opponents aren't more dignified."

## 65. Tucson - Shopping

Joshua is back in Tucson. He walks into the Cotton Mill, the haberdashery where his father used to buy all his clothes. He starts trying on dress shirts. He decides on a long-sleeve dress shirt with French cuffs. He buys six. He tries on a few suits before finding one that fits perfectly, a British cut, double breasted. He buys two in blue, two in dark grey, and two in dark brown. The pants need to be shortened. After choosing a dozen ties, he picks out two pairs of wingtip boots, one black and one brown, with matching belts. Like always, he pays for everything in cash.

"Thanks again. I'm having breakfast with an old friend tomorrow and will swing by afterwards to pick up the suits."

"See you then, Sir," responds the shopkeeper. "If you don't mind me asking, aren't you Christopher Stone's son?"

"I am, Mr. Carson. Great memory. Always nice to visit your store and buy such nice things."

"Hope you don't mind me asking. But you look terrible. Is everything okay?"

"I got into a political discussion two days ago with the wrong people. Those politicians are ruthless."

## 66. Visiting the Texter

The doorbell rings. Giovanni looks up from his morning coffee, slightly confused, and walks to the door. "Who could that be this early in the morning?" He opens the door to Joshua Stone and freezes in shock.

"I'm not here to hurt you. Promise. I just want to talk. May I come in for some coffee?"

Still in shock, the Texter invites Joshua in and makes him a cappuccino. Joshua is glad that at least one thing is going well so far.

"I guess I knew this day would come. I'm sorry for killing your family. It wasn't on purpose. But for sure it was my fault. I think about them every day. I'm so sorry."

"I need to say 'I'm sorry,' too. I had no right to break into your house and threaten you. I'm better than that. I'm sorry."

"I deserved it. Don't worry. I was going to try to keep that secret for the rest of my life. Had you not threatened me, I never would have fessed up. Although two years in prison was unbearable, at least I'm no longer living a lie."

The men sit in silence for a few minutes. Joshua interrupts the silence. "Tell me about your new company."

"The day I got out of prison, I walked into the chamber of commerce and started a nonprofit that partners with local sheriff departments and the highway patrol offices to brief high school kids on the horrors of car crashes resulting from drunk driving, texting, falling asleep at the wheel, and reckless driving. I gave my first brief last month to the local high school and have a brief scheduled for every week for the remaining school year.

"I can't go back in time to save your family. But perhaps I can help young kids see the importance of driving safely. And in doing so … who knows how many accidents I can prevent?"

Joshua nods in approval. Emotions are boiling up within and his eyes start to water. The two men sit in silence for another minute.

Joshua wishes him well with his new life and thanks him for the coffee.

## 67. *National News: America 1ˢᵗ Wins in the Supreme Court*

"The America 1ˢᵗ political party won a huge victory today in our nation's highest court. They were challenged by the Democratic National Committee who claimed that the America 1ˢᵗ political party's system was unconstitutional. Harvard Law School Professor Skip Goldberg represented the America 1ˢᵗ political party. Arguments were heard last week, and the unanimous decision was made this morning. The America 1ˢᵗ political party may be constitutional, but it's prospects for success in the upcoming election are still dismal at best. Republican and Democratic candidates both agree that the A1 candidates don't have a chance."

## 68. *October 1st Arrives*

Finally, October 1ˢᵗ arrives. Joshua calls Robby and Rafael.

"Hey boss, you're not going to believe this," says Rafael.

"Of course, he is going to believe this," interrupts Robby. "He's been planning this the entire time. I know it."

"Ok, boss," continues Rafael, "We did it. We have thirteen million members of our political party. We got enough petitions signed so that our party's candidate will be typed onto the ballot of every state but California. We had eighty-three nominees. And the person who scored best on the leadership assessment is you."

Joshua smiles. "Guys, you had to know that I designed the leadership assessment to give me 100 percent. Mathematically, it would have been impossible for anyone else to have even come close. So, who came in second?"

"The next closest guy is 98 percent identical, but we think he is lying. His timeline just doesn't add up. Plus, he is a career politician who didn't get the Democratic nomination. Third place is the owner of Brayden's Hardware. Fourth place is the owner of multiple banks throughout the world. This guy has great kung fu. He is totally off the grid. Almost untraceable. We're almost positive second place is a fraud, so Brayden's Hardware will likely be your Vice."

"Great work, guys. Send me their bios and I will read them later this morning. I'll call you in a couple of hours to make travel plans."

Joshua jumps onto his e-bike, pedals to the post office, and drops off eleven Federal Express envelopes.

## 69. San Francisco – October 2nd

Although Joshua always preferred to drive, this time he had to fly to San Francisco. He couldn't afford the drive time between vice presidential interviews. It wasn't that Joshua was afraid of flying, it was that he liked to be in control. As a passenger in a plane, he couldn't control any variables. He was just along for the ride. He was powerless. Thankfully, the flight to San Francisco was uneventful.

Joshua drives his rental car, a white Toyota Prius, to the front doorstep of Mark Riley's mansion. Riley is tip-top, dressed in a suit and tie. He gives a condescending look as Joshua introduces himself as the "advanced party" of the America 1st political party.

"Thanks for coming," said Riley. "I expected something more. Where are the leaders of the political party? The camera crew? Did I win? Who is going to be my vice president?"

"Mr. Riley, I will tell you that you did make it into the top ten. It is just protocol that we verify your answers on the leadership assessment face to face before we go on to the next step. Is there a place where we can talk for a few minutes?"

Riley walks him into the living room.

"Hey Babe, you can go. It's no one important. Just some support guy coming to confirm all of the finalists."

A disappointed wife, possibly half his age, flips her hair extensions and walks out of the room.

"Sorry you guys got all dressed up for nothing." Joshua explains. "Perhaps you can start with your family. Was that your daughter, Amber?"

"No, that is my wife, Anne. Amber is away at the university right now."

"Oh. Forgive me," Joshua laughs to himself. "And how long have you been married?"

"Four years."

"Oh, that is weird. Your leadership assessment said that you have been married for over twenty years. Why would you write that?"

Mr. Riley was not used to people talking to him in such an accusative tone. "You better watch your tone with me. What did you say your name was? What business is it of yours if Anne and I have been married for four or twenty years? We love each other. This doesn't affect my ability to lead our country."

"You're right, Mr. Riley. Your love for your wife doesn't change how capable you are to lead a country. But lying about it on a leadership assessment certainly shows that as a person, you're not honest. And dishonesty does affect your ability to lead a country."

Joshua smells blood and decides to escalate: "What else did you lie about, Mr. Riley? Have you ever filed for bankruptcy?"

"That is none of your damn business!"

Mr. Riley takes a few seconds to gain his composure.

"But to answer your question, about ten years ago I made several bad investments. We lost everything except the house. I had to file bankruptcy."

"Mr. Riley, I don't understand why you wrote on your leadership assessment that you've never filed for bankruptcy when, in fact, you have filed for bankruptcy. The America 1ˢᵗ party wants leaders who have integrity, and who are honest. Men who have the discipline to follow through with what they promise. Men who pay their bills and know how to budget. If you can't run a company, how can you run a country? You're a joke. Shame on you."

Riley explodes. "Get out of my house! Get out now! How dare you come and insult me in my own house. I am going to sue you for everything you are worth! You're ruined! I'm going to destroy you!"

*Join the club,* thinks Joshua as he stands up and calmly walks to the door. *Hope this situation doesn't escalate.*

Riley follows him closely. "Everyone knows I should be the next President of the United States, and everyone knows that the America 1st party is my ticket. Who cares if I exaggerated a few things on my resume? America needs a leader who knows how to get stuff done. And what if I didn't lie on that questionnaire? What if I just made a typo?"

"Well in that case, Sir, we still wouldn't want you. Any man who is too incompetent to accurately fill out a questionnaire for something as important as being a presidential candidate doesn't deserve our support. Not to mention that you were given an opportunity to verify your answers at the end of the questionnaire. But you were likely too busy to do it properly."

"Listen, office boy, if your boss doesn't call me tonight and beg for my forgiveness, I promise that I will attack you and the America 1st party with every lawyer in California. And that is a promise. You understand me, boy?"

Riley aggressively grabs Joshua by the arm and swings him around.

"Mr. Riley," Joshua says in a calm voice as he tries to decide if he should escalate the situation or not.

"I understood every word of your message, dare I call it a threat. The problem is, we have already established that you are a liar. So how can I take anything you say seriously?"

Mark Riley takes a step back and throws an amateur swing at Joshua.

Joshua ducks the punch and instinctively retaliates with three almost-instantaneous kidney punches. As Riley bends over in pain, Joshua kicks him in the face. His nose explodes as he flips in the air, landing on his back.

Joshua bends down and whispers in Riley's ear, "I don't like people touching me. And for sure not a lying dirtbag like you. Consider the broken nose a payback for wasting my time with your stupid lies."

Joshua confidently gets into the rental car and bursts out laughing.

*It was a bit too Hollywood,* he thinks to himself as he drives away. *But still kind of fun.*

Once Joshua gets a few minutes down the street, he pulls the car over and takes his cell phone out of his jacket. He presses a few buttons and the entire conversation with Riley starts playing.

*It was a good idea to record that conversation. I'm sure I will need this in the future.*

## 70. Invitations

Eleven Federal Express envelopes arrive to the homes or offices of eleven remarkable people. Every envelope has a handwritten letter, round-trip tickets to Flagstaff, a paid rental car confirmation number, and a paid hotel reservation confirmation number for the Grand Canyon Lodge.

Skip Goldberg is in his office when his secretary brings in the envelope. His eyes get big as he reads. He starts shaking his head up and down. His eyes water.

Mike Campos is at home when the envelope arrives. He hops onto the couch and opens it. A few seconds later, he starts giggling and calls his wife over. She sits on the couch next to him. He shows her the letter. A few seconds later, she starts to cry.

Professor Peter Garcia of Northern Arizona University opens his envelope from his desk. He looks confused, but keeps reading. His face gets brighter and brighter. He smiles, shaking his head up and down.

Lieutenant Colonel Phil O'Connor is at St. Mere Eglise Drop Zone at Fort Bragg. He is observing training. His adjutant hands him the daily mail. He opens the Federal Express envelope first. He laughs and shakes his head sideways. Unbelievable.

Recently retired Brigadier General John Morrison opens his letter from his condo in Vail. He sits on the couch with his wife. He has a few days of facial hair and there are unpacked boxes all around him. They read the letter together. He looks at his wife and shrugs his shoulders. They both start to laugh.

Dr. Stevie Jefferson's assistant hands the doctor his envelope. He sets it on his desk and finishes treating his patient, a seasonal worker with a large cut on his hand. Dr. Jefferson opens his envelope. He smiles and begins to laugh, shaking his head up and down.

Colonel Sean Abbot is at his desk at SOCOM when his secretary brings in the mail. He opens the envelope last, reading it twice. He frowns and shakes his head sideways in disagreement. He knows all the hard work this is going to entail.

Larry, Priscilla, Robby, and Rafael get their envelopes. Larry and Priscilla are in the Jackson Hole office. Robby and Rafael are in their D.C. apartment, which looks more like a server room for an industrial-sized computer network. Although they were already on the team, they knew that receiving this envelope meant that the plan was a success.

Robby looks at Rafael. "Looks like we are going to the Grand Canyon."

## 71. National News: Democrat Leader Indicted for Larson and Assault & Battery

"With the election just five weeks away, the U.S. Democratic Candidate Senator Johnson is getting the worst news imaginable. His chief of staff of eleven years, Mr. Benedict Bruser, has been indicted for conspiracy to commit Arson, Larceny, and Assault & Battery.

"Video evidence from the America 1ˢᵗ security cameras show two men breaking into the headquarters in Jackson Hole, Wyoming, stealing a laptop, and setting the office on fire, making it look like an accident. The two men have been positively identified as Ken Seglyn and Craig Veranom. The laptop's camera, GPS data, and illegally downloaded data filled with trackable blockchain code placed the computer at the home of Mr. Bruser. Furthermore, Craig and Ken were recorded beating an American 1ˢᵗ volunteer at the America 1ˢᵗ headquarters last week. The video is graphic, and not able to be released to the public. But at one point, Ken threatens the volunteer to pull out of the race or he will burn the building down again, this time while people are in it.

"The bigger question is how will this affect Senator Johnson? Did he know about the arson and larceny? Or is he simply guilty of employing a rogue Chief of Staff?"

## 72. Fort Worth: The Ranch

After getting lost five times, Joshua finally arrives at his destination, the middle of nowhere. It is a large country home. "The ranch," perhaps ninety years old, is surrounded by hundreds of acres of farmland. Jimmy Brayden greets Joshua at the front door and introduces himself and his wife, Linda.

"Come on in. Can I get you a cup of coffee?" she says in a typical West Texas drawl.

"Please. Thank you."

"Find us all right?" Jimmy says with a smile.

"Not even close. I don't think GPSs work out here, and for sure, your neighbors were all playing dumb. You have them well trained not to give directions."

Jimmy giggles. "We like people. Actually, we love people. But we just don't like people at our house. Home is for dear friends and family. Strangers can stay away. That is why I have an office, you know?"

Joshua and Jimmy hit it off immediately. Jimmy is fifty-two years old, stocky, salt and peppered, with honest eyes and the crushing handshake of a stone mason. Although Joshua is anxious to get to work, to conduct his unofficial interview, he allows Jimmy to steer the conversation. Jimmy understands the importance of this interview and spends the next few hours telling stories that show what kind of man he is, what kind of leader he is. Joshua is paying attention to everything and notes how Jimmy's priorities are clearly his family and faith. Business is important, but not his priority. Now that his kids are adults, he is free to focus his time on his business. He ran Brayden Hardware honorably and efficiently. And although he is known to be the best boss in America, with the best business practices, he doesn't suffer fools.

"We don't like knuckleheads here in Texas. If you work hard, then you are rewarded. If you are lazy, then you're replaced. At the end of the day, I want my employees to have a good work environment, good pay, and great benefits."

Joshua tells Jimmy about how his employees helped install his solar power system at the cabin and replace the bathroom and kitchen in D.C.

After a few cups of coffee, Jimmy gives his wife a glance, the kind of subtle glance couples who have been married for decades use to silently communicate, and they both nod their head. He invites Joshua to stay for dinner and the evening. Joshua accepts.

During dinner, Jimmy explains that his employees nominated him for the American 1ˢᵗ political party and that if this "crazy idea" worked, he couldn't be worse than the other options on the ballot. Although he wanted to retire in five years, if needed, he would work for the government for eight. His oldest son is more than capable of taking over the business.

Joshua tells Jimmy a little about his history and the death of his wife and son. Linda starts to cry and gives her condolences. Joshua then explains his America 1ˢᵗ project: the leadership assessment, the team he has found, and how he got the party put onto the ballot in forty-nine states. He thinks they would be a good team and that together they would be able to make some very good changes that could really help America and Americans.

Full of nervous energy and excitement, Joshua and Jimmy stay up late, talking policy and tactics. Linda occasionally sticks her head into the room to freshen up their coffee or to give her insight on the topic of the hour. Joshua is impressed with the integrity and simplicity of both of their political ideas. This is going to be a great friendship.

After breakfast burritos at the ranch, Jimmy leads Joshua down some dirt trails into a small town no one has heard of. He stops his truck and points towards the barbershop across the street. Joshua waves, then parks his rental car. After a fifteen-minute wait, Joshua gets a haircut and a shave. It's the first time he has been cleanshaven in almost three years. He leaves a big tip, gets back into the rental car, and drives to the airport.

"Enough manscaping. Time to get to the Grand Canyon."

## 73. National News: America 1st Set to Reveal Candidates

"The America 1st political party has promised to reveal their Presidential and Vice-Presidential candidates later this week. Although all reputable political analysts unanimously agree that they don't have the slightest chance to get elected next month, curiosity is growing. Will their candidates be famous YouTubers, or sports stars with millions of viewers and followers, or will they actually be capable leaders? All are curious. Most are skeptical. We will keep you posted as the reveal gets closer."

## 74. The Grand Canyon

October 9th - Breakfast for the team started at 0900 in the large conference room of the Grand Canyon Lodge. Joshua arrives a few minutes early to find the entire team already there. The excitement is exceptional. Joshua thanks everyone for coming and quickly explains the timeline of events for the next three days.

After breakfast, they make official introductions. All of the married men travelled with their wives. Robby and Rafael brought their girlfriends. And Priscilla brought her husband. Joshua describes the process he used to create the America 1st political party and Larry explains how he legitimized the political party and got them onto the ballot. Priscilla, Robby, and Rafael explain the atypical campaigning strategy they are going to use during the remaining four weeks before the election. The group adjourns after lunch and everyone goes for a long walk along the rim of the Grand Canyon. Dinner is catered in the conference room. BBQ.

October 10th - After breakfast, Joshua and Jimmy meet with each member of the team to discuss highlights for what they want to do to change the government and to help the people over the next eight years. In the afternoon, everyone dresses up, and Priscilla's crew films their first and only promotional video to be aired later that week. Dinner is catered. Mexican.

October 11th - Joshua starts a discussion about operational security and safety, reminding everyone that on Friday afternoon, when their press release airs, they will instantaneously become the most popular people in America. In true military fashion, Joshua makes every member of his team back brief him on the security precautions they are going to take to keep themselves safe. After some final remarks, the team disperses and flies home to prepare for the coming storm.

## 75. *The YouTube Reveal*

Friday at three p.m., Eastern Standard Time, the America 1st political party makes a press release explaining the results of the nomination process and leadership assessments. It announces the names of their Presidential and Vice-Presidential Candidates.

Ten minutes later, the America 1st political party releases its campaign video onto YouTube, the so-called "Grand Canyon Video." It goes viral with over one million views in the first hour and 14 million views that day. Conventional and internet media outlets explode. For the next three days, there is talk of nothing else.

The video consists of the entire team in single file with the Grand Canyon in the background. Joshua introduces himself first.

"Greetings, I'm Joshua Stone, the next President of the United States. I spent twenty years serving the United States in uniform, retiring three years ago as an Army Special Forces Green Beret Lieutenant Colonel. I have the world's best education. I have undergone the world's hardest training. I'm not a politician, I'm a leader. And this is what our country needs. A leader.

"But because a leader is only as strong and as effective as his team, let me have my team introduce themselves. This way, you know who you are getting and what you are getting when you cast your vote on election day. Let start with our Press Secretary."

"Greetings, my name is Priscilla Kartoff. I'm the marketing manager for the America 1st political party and will be the White House Press Secretary. I will give media outlets appropriate access to our Administration but will not tolerate disrespect. We have a hard job to do. Gone are the days when the news cycle runs the White House."

"My name is Dr. Roberto Herz. I studied programming and cybersecurity at MIT and have served at the NSA and Cyber Command for the past seven years. I will run the White House's Cyber Crime division. We believe in a free internet, but not a safe haven for cybercriminals, terrorists, pedophiles, and money launderers."

"My name is Rafael Luvchowsky, criminal justice and cybersecurity expert. I'm also single. I hate bad guys who think they can use the internet as a venue for fraud and have been using my kung fu to put scumbags in prison for years. #nowheretorun."

"My name is Professor Samuel Goldberg. I'm fifty-four years old, married to my high school sweetheart. We have three adult kids. I have been teaching at Harvard Law School since I was twenty-eight. I will be the White House Legal Advisor."

"Hello, my name is Larry Whitfield and for the past seventeen years I have been a lawyer fighting for the environment. I look forward serving as the Chief Administrator of the Environmental Protection Agency. Nothing is more of a priority to me than protecting our natural resources and environment."

"My name is Dr. Peter Garcia and I am the Dean of Students at the Northern Arizona University. I love school and believe that America should have the smartest students in the world. I've dedicated my life to helping students and look forward to serving our nation as the Secretary of Education."

"Hello. My name is Phil O'Connor and I have also served our nation in uniform for twenty years. I am organized, honest, regimented, and consequent. It will be my honor to continue my service as the next Secretary of Defense. Nothing would make me happier than getting members of the military the training and the equipment they need to accomplish their mission."

"My name is Colonel Sean Abbot and I am also a soldier. Don't worry, I am not the tough guy, I'm the smart guy. For the past fifteen years, I have worked at Special Operations Command in the finance section. The Army sent me to Syracuse University to get a PhD in finance. It's not rocket science. If you have a million dollars, you budget and spend less than the million dollars. Then you create a surplus, not a deficit. I don't understand how these idiots in Washington D.C. don't know how to balance a checkbook. This is a skill we all learned when we were kids. I will be the Secretary of the Treasury. I will balance our budget. I will erase our deficit. And I will make the U.S. Dollar the strongest currency in the world."

"My name is Brigadier General John Morrison. Of my twenty-seven years in uniform, I have spent over twelve years serving outside the country. I have worked with U.S.

Embassy personnel and out of U.S. Embassies in thirty-one nations. I speak four languages. Although I am honest and direct, I also know how to work and play well with others. I look forward to serving as your Secretary of State for the next eight years."

"I'm Dr. Stevie Jefferson. I went to Medical School at Vanderbilt, served in the U.S. Air Force for six years, and started two medical practices in Memphis. One is for rich people at the Baptist University Hospital and one is for poor people downtown. I have a passion for helping people, and I take my Hippocratic Oath seriously: to serve and heal. It is an honor to be the next Secretary of Health and Human Services."

"I am Army Special Forces Sergeant Major Mike Campos. I have worked with Joshua all over the world for the past twenty years. I will be the White House Chief of Staff."

"I'm Vice Presidential candidate Jimmy Brayden. Born and raised in West Texas, I started a lumber factory with my father when I was sixteen. With the exception of the year I spent in Vietnam, I've never known another job. We now have 300 hardware stores in fifty states. I manage 12,000 employees, with 31,000 family members. My company makes about 35 million dollars profit a year. I keep 1 percent and give the other 99 percent back to my employees, back to my business, or to honorable charities. I've lived in the same house my whole life, although Linda and I put in a pool last year. I drive an eight-year-old pickup. I promise to take as good of care of the country as I do of my business and employees, and to not take advantage of my position. People come first. I suspect all of you would appreciate it if the government spent your tax money a bit more wisely. Me too. And that is why I am going to focus on the budget and Social Security."

Joshua returns to the screen. "As you can see, the America 1st political party has come through with its promise. It is an honor to be its first candidate for President and the leader of such a distinguished group. Vice President Brayden and I have built a first-class team, a world-class team. America deserves to be run by leaders, not politicians. By men and women with character, not characters. We don't need to announce our cabinet positions until we are officially elected. But we wanted to share with your our most important team members so their credibility will help our credibility. Tomorrow, we will release everyone's full biography. Next week, we will conduct a question and answer session aired on YouTube. November 1st we will publish our eight-year strategy for putting America 1st. And November 3rd is the election. We look forward to serving you and thank you in advance for your vote."

"America 1st."


## 76. *The Next Phase*

With phase one now complete, phase two begins with an interview in a small but elegant library. The ceiling is twenty feet high; the walls are forest green with dark wood bookshelves from floor to ceiling. Two well-worn leather couches face each other in the middle of the room, separated by a marble coffee table with intricately carved legs.

An impeccably groomed Joshua Stone, dressed in a dark suit, sits on one of these old leather couches. Although most of his life and career was spent in anonymity, on this special day in history, all the world's eyes are on him. He is the most famous and newsworthy person on the planet.

Priscilla sits across from him, with a tripoded camera over her shoulder.

There is an air of excitement and joy in the room. You immediately notice the intensity and purpose in the bright eyes of the king sitting on his couch. But if you look hard enough, you can also see a hint of loneliness and sadness.

"What an amazing journey," she begins. "Do you want to tell us how it all concluded?"

Joshua lets loose a humble smile. Sorrow flickers for just an instant as he takes a few seconds to put his thoughts together.

In his characteristically soft and scratchy voice, Joshua slowly begins, "Obviously our YouTube video was a big hit and the campaign strategy was highly successful."

"Senator Johnson was vindicated from his Chief of Staff's sabotage, but for sure it hurt his credibility and it clearly reflected in the polls."

"The sitting Republican President challenged the election results, as we knew he would. But we all know how that turned out …"

A young man respectfully interrupts from the back of the room: "It's time."

"Thank you, Robby. Let's get to work."

## 77. *The Inauguration*

Joshua leaves the room, walks down a long hallway, and out onto a balcony where thirty people are sitting, including all of the members of his new cabinet. Joshua places his hand on the bible and repeats the following oath of office: "I, Joshua Stone, do solemnly swear to up hold the Constitution of the United States of America. To faithfully execute the duties of the President of the United States …"

A vast crowd of people are applauding in the audience ... and all over the world.

## 78. *Let's Get to Work ...*

America 1st - What would you do if you had the rest of your life to change your world?



America 1st / Paperback -- 1st ed.
ISBN: 978-1-946373-09-0
$13.99

www.ingramcontent.com/pod-product-compliance
Lightning Source LLC
Chambersburg PA
CBHW050542190726
48284CB00003B/1178